A SECRET WISH

The earl smiled at Miranda for the first time that day as Julian left them. "I fear we are in for a rare trimming from Aunt Agatha."

Miranda felt a warmth flood through her as she gazed up at his handsome countenance. "She must know you did your best to keep the dog contained in the stable, for I heard your mother ask Julian about it in your aunt's presence."

In a spontaneous gesture Miranda placed her hand on his arm. The earl gazed down at her, studying her with deep intensity. Feeling unable to respond to his nearness, she took a step back to get her emotions in hand. Inadvertently, she lost her balance and began to fall backwards.

With a fluid movement, the earl prevented her from toppling. His strong hands sent strange sensations through her as he clutched her waist and drew her back to him. She trembled with excitement at the feel of his touch even through her thick layers of clothing.

Cresswood's expression stilled as they stood face to face with his hands still resting at her waist. Miranda's heart pounded so strongly, she thought she would faint. His eyes dropped to her lips and she sensed he would kiss her. Tilting her face up towards him, she eagerly waited . . .

Books by Lynn Collum

A GAME OF CHANCE
ELIZABETH AND THE MAJOR
THE SPY'S BRIDE
LADY MIRANDA'S MASQUERADE

Published by Zebra Books

LADY MIRANDA'S MASQUERADE

Lynn Collum

Zebra Books
Kensington Publishing Corp.

http://www.zebrabooks.com

ZEBRA BOOKS are published by

Kensington Publishing Corp.
850 Third Avenue
New York, NY 10022

Zebra and the Z logo Reg. U.S. Pat. & TM Off.

First Printing: May, 1999
10 9 8 7 6 5 4 3 2 1

Printed in the United States of America

Admired Miranda!
Indeed the top of admiration, worth
What's dearest to the world!
—*The Tempest*
William Shakespeare

One

The stable door hinges groaned in protest as Lady Miranda Henley pushed the weathered oak portal open just wide enough to lead her grey Arabian through. She tried to make as little noise as possible as she juggled her reticule and bandbox in her other hand. She could see torches bobbing through the trees around the manor house. No doubt her stepbrother Sylvester had wakened the servants to find her, but how had he known she was gone so soon?

She pulled Baruq to the mounting block, then secured her case and bag to the sidesaddle. Glancing back, she could see the torches moving in her direction now. She scurried atop the block and settled herself securely on the saddle. With trembling fingers, she tied the ribbons of her old poke bonnet over her loose blond curls. She wore a simple blue wool traveling gown instead of her normal riding habit. Having no luggage save her bandbox, she could ill afford the luxury of the habit.

Lady Miranda urged the horse forward, hoping the mare would live up to her Arabic name and run like lightning. A gift from her late uncle, General Joshua Henley, the animal had been the only bright spot in her life since her mother had died and left her under the guardianship of her stepbrother.

The mare was at a fast canter by the time horse and rider turned the corner of the drive. Miranda could see the red of Major Caldwell's tunic in the torchlight and knew at once he was the reason she'd been discovered missing. Her unwanted fiance had come to call and she'd been sent for.

Walking alongside Sylvester, a menacing look on the soldier's leathery face, Major Caldwell advanced on her. The men, childhood friends, had hatched the plot to get Miranda's inheritance, but she would not go willingly into a loveless marriage.

With a light touch of her crop, she urged Baruq into a full gallop, aiming the horse's thundering hooves straight at the major. She thought the man a coward, and wasn't surprised when he fell back in the face of the hurtling animal.

The crowd scattered as she swept through them. Hands grabbed at her and unintelligible shouts were raised, but she merely locked her limbs tighter on the sidesaddle, crouched low, and urged Baruq to lengthen her stride. Within minutes she passed through the gates of Brownstone, leaving behind her stepbrother and all his plots and plans.

The silvery full moon lit her way well enough to throw caution to the winds. She rode her little mare hard for nearly an hour, the cold biting at her cheeks, but she paid little heed. She did not fear for Baruq. The general had once told her a story about a messenger riding for a day and a half nonstop on his Arabian stallion. The man safely delivered his dispatch, then collapsed and died from exhaustion, while his stallion was hale and hearty. They were animals bred for endurance, and she would test Baruq's this very night.

Bringing the horse to a cooling walk, Miranda listened for pursuers, but there were no hoofbeats in the cold night air. She then began to calculate how long it would take her to get to London. If her luck held and everything went according to her plans, she would be at Missy's rooms before sundown the following evening. If not, she would need to find a safe haven, a place where Sylvester could never find her. With a little prayer for luck, she set the horse at an easy canter north.

Having completed a successful night at the tables, Charles Benton, sixth Earl of Cresswood, strolled out of the gaming room at White's. Accompanied by his cousin, Colonel Daniel Turner, the earl paused to don his great-coat against the dawn's chill. His gaze fell upon a plump young man with thinning red hair who wore a rumpled black superfine coat and an intricate white cravat marred by brandy stains.

Cresswood frowned as he recognized Sir Peter Weldon. His old friend slumped in a chair in the outer room, an empty bottle of brandy before him.

Turning to the colonel, Cresswood pointed out the gentleman. "Shall we see Sir Peter to his town house?"

The retired officer eyed the drunken baronet, a hint of reproof settling in his brown eyes. "Hang it, Charles. I see you are still determined to play schoolmaster to all your acquaintances."

Cresswood frowned. "I don't consider helping a friend

home as enacting the schoolmaster. Besides, I would do the same for you, should I find you thus."

"Find *me* thus! I never get jug-bitten."

"True, but Sir Peter is not made of such stern stuff. He never had a head for wine, even at Oxford."

The colonel took his cousin's word on the matter, for being some ten years older than the two he'd never been at school with them. He followed Cresswood over to the foxed gentleman. Colonel Turner knew it would do little good to argue with Charles once he'd set upon a course.

The earl shook the man. "Peter, wake up, old man. You are going to have a dreadful head in the morning."

The baronet opened a pair of deep green eyes that appeared dazed. At last coming into focus, he slurred, "Is that you, Cress? 'Prised to see the paragon you've become in a place like this."

The former soldier struggled not to smile as he stepped forward to aid the earl. There was a prevailing perception of most gentlemen who knew Lord Cresswood that he had become a bit too proper and upright in recent years. But Daniel knew it was only that his cousin wished to set a good example for young Julian Benton, who only recently had been let loose on Society. "Sir Peter, Colonel Daniel Turner at your service. 'Twas I who dragged Charles to this den of iniquity."

Charles ignored the comment, instead urging Sir Peter to come along home. The baronet at first declined, but when he discovered he'd finished his bottle of brandy, grudgingly agreed to leave.

As the three exited White's into the frosty night, a thin layer of fog swirled around them on St. James's. The dim yellow glow of the gaslights flickered up and down the street. In the distance, the Watch called the hour.

Sir Peter was flanked by his friends, his steps so wobbly he required their sober support. He was considerably shorter than his companions, so they held him under his arms to keep him upright.

The baronet was set upon the task of telling the sad tale of the blighted romance which had driven him to drink.

"I tell you she's a goddess . . . hair of gold . . . smells of lilacs. Beautiful blue eyes . . . sparkle like sapphires. The lips of . . . an angel, so sweet . . . and innocent."

Colonel Turner, a tall, weathered blond, looked over Sir Peter's head at Cresswood. With eyes full of amusement he asked, "Do we walk this pathetic lad to Portman Square, or shall we whistle up a hackney?"

"I think it best we walk him home. I, for one, don't wish to be in a carriage with him should he decide to cast up his accounts. Besides, the morning air most certainly shall do him some good." The earl smiled as they led Weldon in the direction of his town house.

"I tell you . . . my Mary is the woman the poets have 'mortalized," Sir Peter slurred. "I'm sure . . . that mushroom of a brother . . . made her leave."

The gentlemen struggled to keep him upright while he spoke.

"More likely, the 'lady' was sure she had already picked her prey clean," Cresswood remarked cynically to the colonel. While he was no prolifigate, he'd discreetly had his fair share of ladybirds and widows and knew they were alike where funds were concerned.

Sir Peter struggled in anger against Cresswood's supporting hold. "No . . . she's not like that. My Mary wants only . . . to save her brother from the . . . cent-per-centers. The paperskull . . . terrible gamester. Haven't wanted to tell her he's bad *ton* . . . forever trying to take me to some gaming hell he frequents. She didn't ask for . . . five hundred pounds—I gave it to her."

Colonel Turner gaped at Weldon in astonishment. "Upon my word, you gave a lightskirt five hundred pounds? I should say she is a step above the muslin set if she accomplished such a feat."

"You shan't speak of her so, or . . . or I'll call you both out," Sir Peter declared. He tried to straighten up to give his angry words sting, but managed only to stumble and fall against Colonel Turner. "I'm sure she'll be home today . . . wondering why I have not called upon her."

"Pray, what was this fair one's name, Peter?" Cresswood inquired with interest.

"Why . . . Miss Mary Hamilton . . . resides in a snug little cottage just off . . . Clarges Street. Tell you, my dear one is . . . most respectable and genteel . . . a veritable treasure herself."

Neither of Sir Peter's friends commented, struggling to keep the drunken fellow upright. The trio made their way through the nearly empty streets with the baronet muttering incoherently until they arrived at Sir Peter's elegant town house.

The sound of the knocker brought his butler to the door. The servant showed no surprise at his employer's condition. He took his master from the gentlemen and thanked them politely. Sir Peter continued to mutter about visiting his fair Mary even as he disappeared from sight behind the closing door.

Cresswood invited Daniel back to Benton House, and the two men hailed a hackney cab. While the carriage moved west to Grosvenor Square, the colonel asked, "Do you think there's any chance of Sir Peter's being right about this Mary Hamilton? He's so enamored she might try to trap him into matrimony."

"I doubt she is genteel. I suspect she was out for some quick blunt and not into so deep a game as marriage. I never heard of this creature before, but she must be a downy one to have gotten five hundred pounds out of Weldon. The shame is we cannot put Bow Street onto her. Peter willingly gave her the money, so no crime was committed. Hopefully he shall be a wiser man after this experience; that is, once he comes to his senses."

"Yes, and a poorer one. I wonder where she will land next to play her little game? She won't find many as rich as Weldon and so easily able to afford such a sum," the colonel said as they drew to a halt at Benton House.

After paying the hackney driver, Cresswood paused with a thoughtful look. "Perhaps we should pay her a visit. Weldon needs his eyes opened to the drab's true colours, and she needs to be taught a lesson."

Entering the front door held open by the butler, Daniel chuckled. "Lesson! Spoken like a true schoolmaster. My advice is, don't involve yourself so deeply in the man's affairs. He's not your brother and damned well might resent your high-handedness."

Cresswood frowned at his cousin's criticism. "I look out for my friends as I do my family. As for my dear brother, Julian resents nearly every word I utter. 'Tis in the nature of wards to disagree with their guardians, especially when that person happens to be an older brother. My mother keeps telling me to loosen the reins, but I fear it is a hard habit to break after thirteen years of trying to control Father's offspring."

The men surrendered their hats and evening capes to Wicks.

"Aye, you've had a full plate raising your younger siblings."

Lord Cresswood merely nodded his head as he led the colonel into the breakfast parlor, where a large sideboard of tempting delights awaited. Both filled a plate and sat to partake of the fare, engaging in idle small talk about the evening's play until their appetites were satisfied.

While the servants cleared away the dishes, Daniel asked, "How are Aunt Lucilla and Cousin Ellen? I've had no opportunity to visit Oakhill since I returned from India."

"My mother is well at present. Keeping busy and enjoying her friends. She recently returned to Oakhill from a brief visit to Bath and is trying to get Ellen out of the stables. The child is hopeless."

"I don't think Cousin Ellen would appreciate being called a child at the advanced age of fifteen."

"What would you call a young lady who thinks she would enjoy the life of a gypsy instead of her own as the proper daughter of a peer?"

Daniel laughed. "She's like all young ladies, tugging against the restraints that Society imposes on their gender. Don't you remember my own sister often threatened to tread the boards? Now she is happily married with two children. Our Ellen will soon outgrow her foolish notions. But, tell me, how is Julian?"

Lord Cresswood shook his head at the mention of his brother. "He's back at Oxford, after being sent down in the spring. I believe he is single-handedly trying to lame all my cattle before he finishes his studies. Should you pass that way, I warn you he is menacing the roads in the area in an effort to make a name for himself as a notable whip."

Colonel Turner arched one expressive brow. "It sounds like he has little aptitude for studying. Is he still army-mad?"

"He was last summer, but he doesn't mention it anymore since we quarreled about the matter. All I ask is that you not breach the subject around Mother. She is terrified at the possibility he might win some race and use the funds to purchase a pair of colours. I am merely hoping he doesn't get himself into any more scrapes until he gains a little more wisdom. I warned him if he gets caught racing again, he is off to the wilds of Scotland and a long visit with Uncle Sebastian." Cresswood sighed with exasperation.

Colonel Turner eyed his friend and relative thoughtfully over his coffee cup before posing his next question. "And you? I hear you are engaged in an affair with the widowed Lady Bronson."

Cresswood, picking up an apple, paused for a moment before he began to pare it with a small knife. "I fear the young widow's charms have faded of late."

The colonel gave his cousin a worried look. Lord Cresswood had been pursued by every matchmaking mama in England since his father died and left him in possession of a large fortune as well as a title. A handsome young man with black hair and slate grey eyes, his masculine good looks and athletic figure set many hearts aflutter. Charles had grown harassed and jaded by all the attention, and while he attended many of the social functions, he was often seen to leave early in the company of friends, never singling out a particular young lady. He had no interest in taking on the additional responsibility of a wife, for, as he told all who would listen, he still had his younger siblings at home.

"Perhaps you should find yourself a proper bride. It would set a good example for Julian."

"You begin to sound like my mother. I have yet to meet a lady who entices me sufficiently to give up my freedom. I doubt such exists. Furthermore, the last thing I want is for Julian to fall in love and wish to marry. Were he to do so, it would undoubtedly be someone totally unsuitable. The halfling does his all to plague me. There is no rush for either of us to marry. So, my friend, I shall dance at the Cyprian's Ball, if I choose."

Daniel laughed. "If there is any justice in the world, you will meet a lady who will turn your ordered world upside down and set you on your aristocratic ear."

Cresswood sighed, weariness settling in his eyes. "Tell me, Daniel, is it just me, or do you not find the current crop of beauties . . . insipid? I vow, I have not had an intelligent conversation with one of them this Season. Not one. They all seem so vain, so shallow. I think if I were past forty and fat as a walrus, it would be no obstacle as long as I had a full purse and a title to barter with."

Just then the mantel clock chimed, alerting the men

to the lateness of the hour. Daniel rose from the table. "Your problem, Charles, is you look at life as if it were some missed adventure. It comes of having a ready-made family at eighteen. I can tell you adventure is not all one expects. I discovered that in India. Give me a girl who is beautiful, sweet-tempered, and will be happy to stay at home in the country with me if I do not want to come to Town and do the pretty."

"Then I suggest you find yourself some vicar's daughter and settle down to have a house full of brats. It always seems that once ladies get a little Town polish, they want to come up for the Season every year." Cresswood followed the colonel to the door.

"My mother wishes me to come home and take up the reins of the estate now that I have sold out. I may look around for a bride in Yorkshire."

Cresswood offered up a grin. "Then I shall wish you good luck. Give my regards to Aunt Verna. I am off to Oakhill Manor for a few days myself. I shall happily come and dance at your wedding when you send word of the coming event. Just don't expect to come to mine any time in the near future."

After bidding his cousin good-bye, Cresswood stopped at the table in the hall to inspect the correspondence left by the butler. The usual cards and invitations were stacked on the back of the tray; at the front lay two private letters.

A musky scent wafted up from the first missive, a letter sent by Lady Bronson demanding that he call. He dropped the note unfinished to read the second message.

Breaking the seal, he glanced at the writer's name. The Honorable Jasper Folson's signature appeared in bold letters at the bottom, a name unfamiliar to him. The letter quickly came to the point: Lord Julian Benton, of Oakhill Manor, was responsible for damage to Folson's carriage, having forced him into a ditch just outside of Town. He was unable to reach Lord Julian after several visits to his Oxford rooms. Upon being told Lord Cresswood was Julian's brother, Mr. Folson reluctantly felt compelled to bring the matter to his attention.

Cresswood stalked angrily into the library to leave a note for his secretary to investigate the claim. As the pen scratched upon the paper, he decided to travel to Oakhill at once, instead of waiting until the morrow as planned. He suspected that was where his erstwhile brother had disappeared after the accident.

Julian would soon have reason to regret ignoring his brother's orders. Finishing the message, the earl left it on his desk and made his way up to change.

Some hours later, as Lord Cresswood tooled his carriage along the road south, fatigue from the long night at the tables overtook him. He knew he must stop to refresh himself, and what better place than the Grey Swan in East Grinstead? A tankard of their fine ale was just the thing to sustain him until he reached Oakhill Manor and met with his wayward brother.

"Do ye think 'er be dead?" the towheaded five-year-old softly asked, peering at the young woman lying on the fresh hay in the shed behind their cottage.

Slapping his brother on the side of the head, the older boy snapped, "Use yer brainbox, Jacko. If 'er were dead, 'er'd be in the churchyard with a big stone sayin' when 'er died."

"Good thin' her's not dead then, cause Da would blame me. 'E always says I'd break an anvil, if'n we 'ad one. But I never see'd 'er 'afore."

"Me neither." The older boy got a thoughtful look on his freckled face. "I think this 'ere's the lady what the red-faced gent was searchin' fer last night."

"Does that mean us gets the guinea the gent was of-ferin' for 'er?"

The older boy again smacked his younger brother on the side of his head, causing the lad's knit cap to slip to one side. "You think Da is goin' to let us 'ave a guinea? Don't be daft. 'E'll use it fer 'is ownself."

"But I would give you fine lads a farthing if you don't tell anyone you saw me." The girl in the hay sat up as she spoke, causing the brothers to jump back in fright.

"A farthing for each of us," Jacko demanded. The daring boy received another smack from his older brother, causing his cap to fly off to the ground. The child quickly retrieved the article, pulling it back over his pale hair. Oblivious to the bits of straw clinging to the wool, he glared at his older brother.

"I'll do the talkin'," the older boy said. "Like 'e said, a farthing for each of us."

Lady Miranda pretended to consider for a moment. "Only if you show me where I might find a place to buy something to eat *and* promise not to tell anyone you saw me."

The brothers looked at one another and broke into wide grins. The older one said, " 'Tis a deal, miss."

Rising, Miranda brushed the straw from her rumpled traveling gown. She was cold and stiff from the few hours she'd spent in the boys' back shed. Baruq had turned up lame barely twenty miles from East Grinstead. She'd made arrangements for her beloved animal to be safely housed with a kind farmer, promising to send extra funds until she could return to retrieve the horse.

Unable to find reliable transportation, however, she'd resorted to walking to London, but fatigue had finally won out. Her former governess would scold her for her foolhardy flight, but hopefully the aged lady would take Miranda in despite her disapproval.

Time was critical. From what the boys said, she knew her stepbrother, Sylvester, was already searching the roads for her. The scoundrel was determined.

Well, she was equally determined to thwart him. She dug around in her reticule for two coins. All she needed was a place to take refuge until he gave up the search.

"There," Miranda said, placing a coin in each outstretched hand. "Now, will you tell me your names, so I might thank you properly?"

The older boy pulled his own worn knit hat from his brown hair. "I be George, miss, named for the king, bless 'is nicked in the nob 'eart. And this 'ere be Jacko, me brother."

"I am excessively pleased to meet you fine lads." Miranda shook each boy's hand. She wished she could offer them better compensation for their help, but her own funds were frightfully low from paying for her horse's board and there would be few funds until she received her inheritance when she reached five and twenty, some five years hence. Her plan was to find employment.

"What crime did ye commit?" Jacko eyed Miranda warily. "Me da say ye must 'ave stole somethin' from the gent, 'im being so wishful to get 'is mitts on ye."

Miranda gave a bitter laugh. "No, Jacko. I am running from my stepbrother to keep him from stealing my inheritance by selling me to the highest bidder."

"Does that make us 'eroes or somethin'?" Jacko flashed a cheeky grin.

The older boy smacked his brother's head, causing bits of the straw to fly loose. " 'Course not, ye bird wit."

"I beg to differ, George. I shall always consider you lads my heroes for helping me escape." Miranda smiled.

Jacko's tiny chest swelled visibly. "Just like I reckoned."

George gave a light snort and rolled his eyes. "Unless ye wants to get caught, us ought to take ye to the inn 'afore Da comes out 'ere and takes our blunt *and* gives ye up to the gent."

Taking a nervous glance over her shoulder, Lady Miranda picked up her reticule and bandbox. "Lead the way, brave lads, and I shall follow."

The brothers trooped across a snow-dusted field, heading for a stand of trees. Miranda was frozen to the bone from the cold November wind well before they climbed the stile at the edge of the field and entered the woods. The late morning sunshine radiating on her back had helped curb the chill, but that comfort was lost when she entered the dark woods. It would be a risk to go to an inn, but she needed the reviving warmth of a cup of tea and a fire, if she could manage such.

When they came to the edge of the woods, the boys stopped. George pointed to the cluster of buildings

straight ahead. "That be the Grey Swan. Ye can get the
stage to Lunnon from there. Us must be gettin' back
afore Da comes lookin' fer us."

Miranda thanked the boys and watched them disap-
pear back up the trail, George warning his little brother
to keep his coin hidden.

As she turned back to the building, the sounds and
smells of the inn's kitchen reached her, making her mouth
water. She needed sustenance. She might get a seat on the
stage if there was no sign of her stepbrother. Taking a
deep breath of the crisp air, she marched forward.

The Grey Swan was an ancient ivy-covered posting
house set at an angle to the stables. The leaves on the
ivy were brown now, giving the inn a neglected look.
Miranda made her way between the two buildings, pausing at the edge of the inn to survey the busy stable yard.

Curricles and coaches cluttered the area. Several bore
a marked resemblance to Sylvester's small black vehicle,
but she couldn't be certain. While she scrutinized the
yard, her gaze came to rest on a gentleman in conversation with his groom. Miranda was uncertain what drew
her attention to the handsome man, but her eyes lingered
on his elegant figure.

He was tall and well-built beneath his fashionable attire. In the morning wind, black hair ruffled around the
edges of his beaver hat. But what held her attention was
a pair of intelligent grey eyes and a classically handsome
face. She detected touches of humor around his generous
mouth, a trait she found lacking in too many people.

Miranda's heart began to pound when he looked in
her direction. She drew back into the thick vines of ivy,
causing some of the dried leaves to fall to the ground.

She didn't want him to see her in her old-fashioned traveling dress with straw still in her hair.

How foolish, she thought. As if she would ever see the gentleman again. But she remained hidden in the shrubbery, imagining herself in London, dressed in finery and dancing with a gentleman like the one before her.

Her daydream came to an abrupt and frightening end when Sylvester strolled out of the Grey Swan. Her knees trembled as he walked over and addressed the gentleman who'd just been occupying her thoughts.

A wave of disappointment rushed through her when she realized that the handsome man was not only acquainted with her despicable relative, but appeared to know him well.

Edging back from the corner of the inn, Miranda turned and hurried into the woods, making certain to keep the building between her and her pursuer. Her only option was to go west for a while in hopes of evading Sylvester. 'Twas a decided pity about the handsome gentleman being her stepbrother's friend, for that automatically made the man her foe.

The sun hovered just above the tree line as Lord Julian Benton tooled his curricle down the road to Crawley, heading for home. The look of concentration on his face was not due to the intricacies of handling his team, but to how best to get an advance on his allowance from his mother to quiet a certain gentleman farmer near Oxford. Julian felt it would be useless to tell Cresswood the accident was not his fault, for there had been too many that were.

Turning his head slightly, he shouted to his groom, "I think we shall make Oakhill in time for dinner. If I were running at top speed, I could have driven it in an hour less."

Jamie, the groom, only nodded his head in agreement. He was glad Lord Julian had traveled at such a modest pace. He didn't want another trimming from Lord Cresswood.

As Julian returned his attention to his team, they approached a sharp bend in the road. He took the turn easily enough, but a woman ran heedlessly across his path. He saw the white flash of a frightened face, then felt a slight jarring of the carriage as he whizzed past.

Julian hauled on the reins, but the horses, in full flight, fought him every step and it seemed a great distance before he could pull them up. "Get the team, Jamie."

The groom jumped down, running to hold the horses' heads. Julian dropped his reins, leapt down, and rushed back to the ditch where the girl lay, facedown and still.

" 'Ow be the mort, Lord Julian?" Jamie shouted as he walked the horses in a circle and headed back to where the woman lay.

Kneeling beside the victim, Julian did a quick inspection of her limbs. "I don't think there are any broken bones, Jamie, but she is unconscious." He gently turned her on her back. The ribbon on her bonnet had broken, and it fell from her head as she rolled over. Her golden blond hair spilled across the ground. Julian gently brushed the sand from her pale face. She didn't appear to have any outward signs of serious injury except a small nick at her hairline, but her unconscious state frightened him. He needed a doctor to determine her condition.

"We must take her to Oakhill Manor at once. Mother will know what is best to be done." His stomach tightened at the thought of the young lady having been harmed. In all his troubles with driving, never before had he hurt anyone.

While he lifted the senseless woman into the carriage for the short trip to Oakhill, Jamie gathered her bandbox and reticule, stowing them under the seat. Julian felt a tremor of fear run down his back. He wasn't certain if it was for the injured beauty or for himself, for he knew his brother was going to be furious when he learned of Julian's newest mishap.

Lord Cresswood halted at the doorway of the drawing room of Oakhill Manor. Dressed for dinner, he was hoping to see his brother, but a lone person occupied the elegantly furnished room.

Seated in a wing-backed chair was his cousin Amelia, dressed in her favorite colour, grey. She was occupied with her ever-present stitchery. A foolish woman, she had little to recommend her but a lack of bitterness about her situation in life. Her one fault was always imagining herself ill.

"Good evening, Cousin. I am surprised to find you alone."

Upon seeing the earl, the lady jumped to her feet, scattering bits of coloured silk on the Aubusson carpet.

"Lord Cresswood! I did not know you had returned from London."

Coming forward to retrieve the lady's scattered thread, Cresswood signaled his relative to be seated. "I have often told you, Cousin, there is no need for you to stand when I enter the room, and you might call me Cousin Charles."

"As if I would not give you your proper respect," Amelia replied with a girlish laugh. "Well, I know the honour your family has bestowed upon me by allowing me to reside with you. If only I could do more to show my appreciation, but too often I find myself unwell."

"It is not necessary that you work for your lodging, for you are part of the family," the earl replied in a dampening tone. "Have you seen my mother?"

Taking a seat, Amelia went back to setting stitches. "I believe that she is with Lady Ellen. The governess, Miss Clairmont, is away visiting her mother, so the countess is keeping your sister under a watchful eye."

Charles smiled, knowing that his young sister could be quite a handful, but their mother adored her adventurous young daughter and would find it no hardship to keep her company. "Then may I offer you a glass of sherry while we await—"

A dog's incessant barking outside interrupted the earl. Within minutes, a ruckus echoed in the front hallway; then the door to the drawing room was opened by a footman.

Julian appeared in the portal. In his arms, he cradled an unknown female. Her head rested on the boy's shoulder, and her blue gown was covered with mud.

With a sinking feeling, Cresswood realized there had

been an accident. Worse, Julian was most likely responsible.

"What happened?"

Julian halted just inside the room when he spied his older brother. "I swear I wasn't racing, Charles. She just dashed out in front of me and I ran her over. I couldn't avoid her."

The lady lifted her head and blinked her eyes as if she were just coming to her senses. Then, as if the earl's accusatory tone sank into her befuddled mind, in a soft voice, she defended the young man who'd run her down. "He is telling the truth, sir. The accident was—" She halted mid-speech, then at last sputtered out, "N-not his fault."

Julian looked at the lady in his arms. "Thank God, you are awake. I was beginning to fear the worst."

Cresswood stared speechless at the lady his brother held. The injured woman was breathtaking. A mass of golden hair tumbled about her shoulders, framing a lovely oval face with delicate features. Cornflower blue eyes stared back at him in terror, as if she feared they meant to do her more harm. Then he saw a large swelling at the edge of her hair.

"Bring her to the sofa," the earl ordered. He was angry with himself for behaving like a moonling over the merest slip of a girl.

While Julian came toward the gold damask sofa, his dog escaped from where she was being held in the hall. Issuing a sharp bark of joy, she danced around her master.

Cousin Amelia, who'd been quiet throughout Julian's entry, fairly flew out of her chair, her colourful silk thread again flying in all directions. "Oh, dear! Oh, dear!"

Looking back at her, Cresswood was shocked to see his frail cousin now standing behind the wing-backed chair, her sewing clutched to her breast. Her gaze was locked on Ruby, Julian's hound.

"What is the matter, Cousin?"

"Animals," the lady said with great revulsion, "are *great* carriers of disease. You know how weak my constitution is." Amelia shifted the chair a little to make certain the dog could not reach her.

Julian, having deposited the injured lady gently on the couch, turned to stare at the red mongrel, who'd settled comfortably in front of the fire and was docilely gazing from one human to another. In a defensive tone, Julian said, "Ruby has never been sick a day in her life."

Amelia's gaze never left the red dog. "Are—are you quite certain? 'Tis so difficult to tell with an animal."

Cresswood thought his cousin henwitted beyond belief. "We are quite positive, Cousin. Julian, take Ruby to the barn. But order Miller to summon the doctor before you go."

Realizing he was due a scolding for the accident, Julian gladly exited the parlor, whistling for Ruby to follow. The dog bounded after her beloved master.

Miranda sat quietly on the sofa. This was a devilish bad stroke of luck. Here she was in the very house where she would least like to be—with Sylvester's friend. She quietly watched as the gentleman helped the older lady retrieve her silks from the floor.

Miranda's head and left ankle throbbed terribly, and she was so tired she could barely think. She suspected the injuries were severe enough to require her to stay abed for several days, but she knew she must do something to prevent Sylvester's friend from learning who she was. No doubt this man would send word at once that he had recovered the missing stepsister, should he determine her identity.

Clasping the elderly lady's arm, the gentleman came to stand beside Miranda. "Allow me to present my cousin, Mrs. Amelia Warren. I am Charles Benton, the Earl of Cresswood. How are you feeling, Miss . . . ?"

Miranda was frantic. She couldn't tell him her name, but her head hurt so horridly she couldn't think what to do. Mercifully, nature took its course and she fell into a swoon before she could answer.

Lord Cresswood's words were left hanging in the air as the young woman touched her head, then, with a soft sigh, sank into unconsciousness.

The usually fluttery Cousin Amelia was suddenly all in command. "I shall go and have a room prepared for the young lady. Fetch a footman to carry her up the stairs and we shall get her comfortably settled before the doctor arrives. I shall need several servants to assist in her nursing."

Cresswood nodded. His wits were in a bit of a muddle. He wasn't certain if it was the marked change in Cousin Amelia or the effect the lovely young woman on the sofa had on him. He simply followed his relative's orders, with a twist of his own.

Gently picking up the girl, the earl found she was surprisingly light. Her head came to rest on his shoulder, and her golden hair brushed whisper soft against his cheek. The scent of roses and—strangely—hay wafted up from her. There was a sudden warming in his loins. As he followed his cousin up the stairs with his provocative burden, he wondered what the devil was the matter with him.

Two

The following morning, Charles lingered over coffee in the breakfast parlor, waiting for news of the patient. He was glad he'd delayed his confrontation with Julian, except now his brother seemed to have vanished. His mind on his errant sibling, Cresswood watched the sun melt ice crystals from the window until his sister, Ellen, appeared in the doorway.

The earl was startled at how grown-up she looked in a simple pink muslin gown. Her raven locks were curled in tight ringlets above each ear and her grey eyes held a look of surprise.

She hesitated a moment, then said, "Good morning, Charles. I didn't expect to see you still sitting at breakfast."

"I, my dear, have been up since seven. I rode round the estate to see how the bailiff has managed with the orders I left. But why are you down so late? Don't tell me you were hoping to avoid me, too?"

Smiling, she bounded over to hug him, reminding him that she was little more than a child still. "No, but you were in such a foul mood last evening, I was not sure what to expect." After giving him a long look, she took the seat opposite him. "I talked to Julian and I know he is in your black books. Charles, will you not reconsider and change your mind about sending him to Uncle Sebastian's like you threatened last summer? It is so dreadfully dismal in Scotland during the winter."

"Did our brother send you to plead for mercy?" Cresswood asked with amusement while he poured out the hot chocolate the maid had just delivered.

"Oh, no. Indeed, he would be much distressed to know I broached the subject, but he assures me he hasn't had a single race since he lamed your chestnuts." Ellen spread marmalade on her toast.

"Apparently not, if what his groom told me this morning is true. I got the story out of him about the girl and about the gentleman near Oxford. I fear I jumped to the wrong conclusion when I received the man's complaint. You may tell Julian that he does not need to avoid me."

"He is not afraid to see you, you know. It's just that Julian feels guilty someone was harmed because of his driving."

"Perhaps this is a lesson he needed, and he will learn to use more discretion when handling the ribbons. I just pray the young lady is not seriously injured. Have you spoken to Mother this morning?"

"Yes, I stopped in the injured lady's room before coming down. Mother and Cousin Amelia were waiting for Dr. Mason to finish his examination. They're concerned the girl hasn't awakened." She paused before coyly adding, "You didn't tell me she is such a beauty."

"Is she?" Charles sipped his coffee. "Well, it makes no difference. I am more concerned that she recovers and we find out who she is. I cannot conceive what she was doing on the road alone so late."

"Do you suppose she ran away from school? Or maybe she was eloping."

"Since she was alone, I think we can rule out an elopement, and she looks old enough to be out of the schoolroom. Most likely, she was employed as a governess or companion and got turned off suddenly. Lady Ramsey is forever leaving some poor creature stranded at the Wild Boar with little or no money. But this is all just idle speculation. I suggest we wait until she recovers and can tell us something of herself. In the meantime, do you wish to ride with me tomorrow morning?"

"Oh, yes. It is so boring with you and Julian gone so much of the time. The grooms are such slowtops I don't enjoy riding with them." Ellen's grey eyes sparkled with anticipation. "Can we go to the old mill?"

The earl eyed his sister suspiciously. "You have been to the mill dozens of times and it is a very long way. Why would you wish to go again?"

"Julian said there is a band of gypsies camped there and they have several monkeys which are allowed to run free."

Cresswood felt a sudden urge to throttle his indiscreet young brother, but merely replied, "You can see all the animals you wish the next time Mother takes you to London. You know I don't wish you to go near those gypsy camps."

Ellen stared at Charles defiantly. It would be months before Mama went back to London. And the monkeys were here now. But she decided it was a wiser course to change the subject than to argue with her stubborn brother. "I am very pleased with the new mare you bought me in September. Did you know I raced Jeremy Evers to his father's manor and beat—"

"Ellen, no gently bred lady races her horse. It is one of the rules of Society that you must learn to obey."

"Oh, Charles, don't you scold me, too. Mother has been going on and on about rules. I think Society has a rule for every occasion and most of them spoil any hope of having fun." Lady Ellen pouted prettily.

Cresswood reached over to pat her hand. "I know you find it difficult to understand at your age, but we all have rules to live by. For Mother's sake, I hope you will learn to follow them and make her proud. Now, I have estate accounts to attend to. I'll see you at nuncheon."

Cresswood stood and kissed his sister on top of her head as if she were five instead of fifteen. "Ask Mother to inform me what the doctor has to say about our guest."

Leaving his sister alone, he exited the small parlor. About to enter the library, he turned instead and went up the stairs to the Blue Room where the injured lady was housed. He wasn't certain what drew him. Perhaps it was merely to ascertain if the woman was truly as beautiful as he remembered, or merely to know her name.

About to knock, he stopped himself. This was ridiculous. She was a stranger. He had no business being fascinated with some nameless chit. Forcing his hand back to his side, he turned and strode immediately to the library, where he belonged.

For the next hour, Cresswood labored over the account books left by his bailiff, but he found it difficult to concentrate. Visions of the girl upstairs kept intruding. Instead of columns of figures, he saw a pair of enchanting blue eyes and hair the color of newly minted gold.

Frustrated, he pushed the ledger aside and walked over to the window. Gazing out at the well-manicured lawns, he asked himself why this mysterious young woman was having such an effect on him. Beautiful women were nothing new to him, but not even the loveliest of London's high-fliers had ever caused him to forget what he was about. Perhaps it was her fragile vulnerability. He never could abide seeing a helpless creature hurt. His weakness was well known on the estate. His mother said the tenants took advantage of him—not to mention the advantages Ellen and Julian took.

A knock at the door brought his attention back to the present. He glanced around as his mother entered the room.

A tall woman in her middle fifties, the dowager countess retained traces of her youthful beauty. Her once-dark hair was white, but her hazel eyes were full of life. She smiled sweetly. "Good morning, dearest. How was your ride?"

"Excellent, thank you. The estate is doing well under our new bailiff, do you not agree?" Cresswood held a chair for his mother to be seated, then settled opposite her.

"I do. The tenants seem pleased with him, too. I think you made a good choice when Boggs retired, but I did not come down to discuss bailiffs. Have you seen Julian this morning?"

"No, but I did talk with Jamie, and he assured me that Julian was not racing his carriage. As for the gentleman in Oxford, Mr. Folson, it seems a dog caused my brother's team to shy and threw Julian's carriage into him. So you can take that frown off your face. I shan't send Julian to Uncle Sebastian."

Lady Cresswood smiled at her older son. "I knew you would be fair to Julian, Charles, but I wanted to discuss our responsibility for taking care of this young girl. Dr. Mason cannot be sure of anything until she regains consciousness. He said the longer she remains in this condition, the more serious the matter is. I also worry the young lady's family may be searching for her and we have no clue as to her identity."

"There is little we can do until she recovers. We cannot just blatantly advertise for her relatives. If Ellen were in this situation, we would want whoever found her to use as much discretion as possible. The fact the girl was alone leaves her open to unpleasant gossip."

"I know you're right, dear, but her mother must be frantic with worry—"

Cresswood reached across and took his mother's slim hand in his strong grasp. "Will you feel better if I send someone to inquire at the local inns? If anyone in the neighborhood is asking for her, we should hear."

"Yes, I shall feel better," Lady Cresswood said; then she rose. "Now, I have taken enough of your time and must see about today's menu."

"I am always at your disposal." Cresswood stood and gallantly walked her to the door. "Try not to worry, Mother."

She reached a hand up and lightly touched his cheek. "You're a good son, Cresswood. Both of my boys are."

She left before he could reply, but he knew it was a gentle rebuke for misjudging Julian. Cresswood, deciding to speak with his brother, set out to find him, knowing that most likely the boy had taken refuge in the stables.

In the hallway he spoke briefly with Cousin Amelia, who repeated much of the same information about the patient, then continued his search. Making his way to the stables, he realized that his cousin was suddenly full of good health now that she was nursing the girl.

He found Jamie first. The tiger was talking with several other grooms as they polished tack. Cresswood drew him aside.

"I need you to go to Crawley and East Grinstead. Keep your eyes and ears open. Don't ask any questions, but see if someone is asking about our guest."

Jamie nodded. "Trying to find who the lady belongs to?"

"As discreetly as possible." The earl tossed the groom several coins. "Have you seen my brother?"

"In the stable, my lord."

The earl found Julian in his shirtsleeves, stooping to check the fetlocks of one of the greys he'd driven home. Ruby sat quietly at his feet, chewing on an old strip of leather.

"How is he?" Cresswood asked, leaning against the door of the stall.

Julian stood with a start. His face flushed but he met his brother's gaze gamely. "No problems that I can see. I just wanted to make sure." He patted the grey on the rump and left, carefully latching the door behind him after Ruby also exited the stall. Almost casually, he asked, "Has Dr. Mason left?"

"Yes, but the lady is still unconscious. I just spoke with Cousin Amelia. She is taking care of the girl, following Mason's directions. I am sure your young lady will be fine," he added as he saw the worried shadows in his brother's eyes.

"I feel like a beast for running her down, but, Charles, I swear I was not racing. I want you—"

Cresswood raised a staying hand. "First, let me say that I talked with Jamie and I know you were not racing. You might want to keep a tighter rein on the greys on sharp curves; otherwise I have no quibble with your driving. As to the other matter, I told my man of business to take care of the bill Folson sent me."

"He sent you a bill? Why, that blackguard! I told him I would send the damned money—"

"Easy, Julian. Apparently Folson went to your rooms and found you had left for Town."

"I was coming down here to borrow the money from Mother, but I stopped for a day with friends in London," Julian admitted sheepishly.

"Borrow! Why? Don't tell me your pockets are to let already? Julian—you aren't gambling, are you?"

"Lord, no. But dash it, Charles, I had to order some new coats. When I saw what they were wearing in Town—well, there was nothing for it but to go to Scott."

"Say no more. I would not want to be responsible for hindering a budding fop." Charles's grey eyes twinkled. They were the exact same shade as his brother's.

"Fop," Julian sputtered until he realized his brother was roasting him. "Well, at least I shan't embarrass you in public."

"So I should hope," Cresswood said as they left the stables. "How long do you plan to stay? There is the matter of your studies."

"I wish to remain until we know how the young lady is. Don't say no, Charles," Julian coaxed as they walked back to the house. "I wouldn't be able to concentrate if I went back now. I shall work hard when I return."

"Very well. Stay, then, until the lady has recovered." Cresswood added, "In the meantime we should concentrate on finding out how to contact her family."

"Oh, well, as to that, Jamie took her bandbox and reticule to the house this morning. We completely forgot about it in the rush to get the doctor."

"Perhaps we might at least be able to discover who she is from them." Cresswood looked down at the hound who trotted at Julian's heels. Remembering Cousin Amelia's reaction to the animal, he said, "I know Ruby is happy to see you, but keep her away from the house."

"She missed me. Mother never gets upset unless Ruby scratches the furniture, and she only does that if left unattended."

"Well, I suggest you visit her in the stables, or Mother will be sending you to Scotland if you get Cousin Amelia all worked up," Cresswood warned, while he and Julian entered a side door of the manor, leaving the sad-eyed dog outside. Ruby barked at her rude exclusion from the house.

Miranda lay in the warmth of the bed. Her head ached dreadfully. With a huge effort she opened her eyes. She was alone in a well-appointed room with flowered wallpaper and blue hangings. Despite the throbbing in her head, she had slept deeply. Closing her eyes again, something began to nag at her brain. With a gasp, she remembered. Somehow she had managed to end up at the home of her stepbrother's friend. She couldn't recall his name or even if he had told her what it was, but his handsome face remained vivid in her mind. She longed to see that face again.

How dreadful to be having such thoughts of her enemy, for that was what he must be if he was Sylvester's friend. She needed a plan. Her injuries would require some time to recuperate and that meant remaining with the handsome gentleman and his family. The problem was if she told them her name, all that would change. Her stepbrother would be summoned and all would be lost. She would be dragged home and forced to wed Major Caldwell.

Hearing a noise outside her door, Miranda was at a loss as what to do or say. Her thoughts were still too muddled to know what was best, so she quickly closed her eyes, feigning sleep. The door opened and closed; then she heard someone's breathing close at hand. A gentle hand felt her forehead; then a female voice muttered, "Good, no fever."

A chair creaked nearby and Miranda knew she had a companion close by should she waken and require something. With a silent sigh, she wished circumstances were different. Clearly, this kind family intended to nurse her back to health, at least until they learned her true identity.

The door opened a second time. "Mrs. Warren, Lord Julian sent these thin's up 'ere. They belong to the young miss."

The lady responded, "Thank you, Sally. I shall be needing you later to sit with our patient. Lucilla insists that I dine with the family."

"I won't be late, ma'am."

The door opened and closed again. Risking a peek, Miranda saw Mrs. Warren had taken her bandbox and reticule. She sat them on a small table covered with a blue cloth.

The lady muttered softly to herself, "Oh, I hope you will forgive me, young lady, but they will want to know your name, so I had best take a look."

Opening the box, the lady took out the silver brushes. Running her fingers over the etched monogram, Amelia made a 'hmmm' sound. Reaching into the case to remove another item, she halted and took out a white piece of paper which was tucked into the top of the box.

Mrs. Warren opened the folded paper and read quietly for a moment, then said, "So you are Miss Mary Hamilton. Cresswood will be pleased I can inform him of your identity, I think."

Miranda tried to sit up and correct the mistake, but as she did so, everything swirled and again she was on the verge of sinking into darkness. When finally her thoughts were more ordered, she realized that Mrs. Warren's mistaking her old governess's name for her own was the perfect solution to her dilemma. Why not use Missy's name, at least until she was recovered enough to leave? She hated the idea of the deceit, but it seemed to be the only way.

Fatigue from her long journey captured her again. Still needing sleep, she was as yet unwilling to face her stepbrother's friend.

Lady Ellen was seated at a mahogany tea table working on a dissected map when the earl entered the drawing room before dinner. Lord Julian, at her shoulder helping her, glanced up to see his brother and blushed to be caught at what he perceived as a childish pursuit. "There you are, Charles. I had begun to think you'd gone back to Town."

Cresswood walked up to watch as his sister set one of the pieces of China in place. "That is a fine map, Ellen. Where did it come from?"

"Cousin Daniel sent it to me when he returned. Have you seen him? Is he as brown as a wren?"

"I thought him a raja when first I laid eyes on him. We must invite him to Oakhill Manor in the new year."

Lady Ellen giggled, then went back to her picture. Soon she and Lord Julian were busy setting pieces while they waited on their mother and Mrs. Warren to join them.

The earl strolled to the window, allowing his thoughts to return to the lady upstairs. He'd spent the afternoon going over the accounts and writing down orders for the bailiff, but continued to worry over their guest. There was still no news from the patient's room. He was hoping to hear the young lady had awakened.

When his siblings fell to arguing over a proposed trip to Crawley, Charles returned to the table. A smile crossed his lips when he at last took note of Julian's yellow coat. Scott may have made it, but the tailor had never suggested that colour. "Julian, words fail me . . . I cannot adequately express my . . . astonishment."

Ellen, seeing her eldest brother sweep Julian with an appraising gaze, said, "He looks like a true Pink of the Ton."

Tugging the bottom of the lemon-hued jacket, Julian straightened. "You don't think it a bit too bright?"

Lady Ellen shook her head, making her black curls sway. "No, you look bang up to the mark."

Cresswood laughed. "My boy, remember you are asking advice from a young lady who thinks merino is the name of a horse. As for you, little one, Mother might prefer you not to use cant such as 'bang up'." His eyes twinkled as he added, "And I doubt you would want to spend an entire quarter's allowance on one coat."

Ellen gazed at the garment with round eyes. "Did you really spend that much, Julian?"

"No, Charles is only teasing. However, I could probably have had three coats made in Crawley for what this one cost."

"True," Cresswood agreed. "But then you would look thrice the provincial." The brothers laughed as their sister stared at them, puzzled.

Lady Cresswood entered the room just as their laughter subsided. The gentlemen waited for their mother to be seated.

"I am afraid there is still nothing new to report about our patient," she said in a concerned tone. "The only good news is she is not feverish. The doctor said that was important. He feels certain that she is merely in a deep sleep."

"Will Cousin Amelia be joining us this evening?" Ellen asked, rising from the table to take a seat beside her mother.

"Yes, but she is probably still changing. I insisted she let one of the maids sit with our guest during dinner."

"Did you find anything in the girl's bandbox or reticule to identify her?" Cresswood asked, ever anxious to know the lady's identity.

The dowager looked stricken. "Heavens, I was so busy with Cook, I simply forgot to ask Amelia. She'll be able to tell us what she found at dinner."

Lord Cresswood glanced around at a discreet tap on the door. The portal opened to admit the butler, Miller, looking very formal and much on his dignity.

"Mr. Reginald Chartley, my lord."

A young man of willowy build and vague countenance strolled into the room. He wore a pale green coat, a canary yellow waistcoat adorned with green flowers, and green striped pantaloons. Black Hessian boots sporting large gold tassels gleamed in the candlelight. Blond hair fell into neatly arranged curls around his thin face. His attire cast Julian's coat into the conservative shadows.

Conscious of his splendor, the sprig bowed before Lady Cresswood, saying with a slight stutter, "M-Must beg your pardon, Aunt Lucilla, for turning up uninvited. Could not write I was arriving. I fear I left Town in a devilish hurry." While he spoke, he eyed himself in the mirror over the fireplace, adjusting the diamond in his cravat ever so slightly.

The members of the family gazed at Reginald with expressions ranging from Ellen's wide-eyed wonder to Julian's patent disgust.

Charles nodded pleasantly. "Good evening, Reggie. What brings you to Oakhill?"

"My new coach. They delivered it yesterday and 'tis positively splendid. Had it done in pale lavender with yellow wheels. M-My coachman informs m-me that it handles superbly."

Cresswood ignored a snort from his brother. "You are welcome, of course, but surely you did not travel all this distance merely to show off your coach."

"M-Marriage," Reggie replied ingeniously. "M-Mama has some new heiress for m-me. Cannot convince her I'm not a m-marrying m-man. Been kicking up a dust for m-me to m-meet this latest one. She invited Lady Sarah to come for a visit. Daresay I should have stayed, but got a glimpse of the lady as she arrived last night. No fashion sense a'tall. Spotty, as well."

"Am I to understand you have defied Aunt Agatha? You are to be commended." Cresswood chuckled with amusement.

Lady Cresswood reproved him. "Charles, I think you would not be amused if either Julian or Ellen flouted your wishes." Turning to her nephew, she added, "You are most welcome to come to us at any time, Reggie, but I must insist you write my sister-in-law and inform her of your whereabouts."

"Write?" Reginald looked at her, horrified. "You cannot m-mean it, Aunt. I told the butler where I was off to. He's sure to tell M-Mama."

"Nevertheless, Reggie, your mother will be less likely to take a pet if she hears from you personally."

Reginald seemed much struck by her words. "Believe you are right, Aunt Lucilla. I shall put some words to paper. She knows what a task it is for m-me and will be greatly m-mollified."

"Very good, Reggie," Lady Cresswood said. "We shall be dining soon. I must have Cook set back dinner thirty minutes to give you time to change. Let Miller show you to your room, while I send word to the kitchen."

Reginald raised his eyebrows. "Thirty minutes! I shall have to build a fire under Gresham. He says he cannot turn m-me out suitably in under an hour." Frowning over the pressure he was under, Reginald followed his aunt out of the drawing room.

As the door closed behind them, Julian said, "Lord, talk about fops! He grows worse every year."

"There is no harm in him. Remember, you might have turned out the same way if Aunt Agatha was your mother. No doubt we shall receive a visit from her in the next few days," Cresswood said as the door opened and his mother came back, trailed by Cousin Amelia.

Mrs. Warren, a distant cousin to the family, had spent much of her life caring for her invalid husband. After his death, she'd come to Oakhill at the dowager's invitation. Now, for the first time since her arrival, she felt truly needed, tending the unfortunate young lady. A soft, happy glow radiated from her thin face.

After greeting his cousin, Lord Cresswood poured her a glass of sherry. When the earl took his seat, he asked, more for the sake of conversation than hope of any news, "How is the patient?"

Amelia, blushing at being the focus of attention, replied with unusual directness. "I am concerned, but Dr. Mason seems to think our patient will wake soon. She has become increasingly restless."

"What of her things? Did you unpack her belongings?" Lady Cresswood leaned forward, remembering the vanity case.

"Oh, yes, indeed. I knew you would wish me to do so, instead of the maid. The girl has a lovely set of silver brushes. I have never seen such workmanship. They reminded me of—"

"Yes, I am sure they were lovely, Cousin Amelia, but did you learn her name?" Charles interrupted, forgetting his manners in his anxiety to learn something of the girl.

Startled, Amelia blinked at him. "As I said, the silver brushes had a monogram on them. The letters M and H were clearly worked into both brushes. Knowing you feel it of the utmost importance to discover her identity, I continued to search and it was there all the time." She paused, waiting for someone to say she had done as she ought.

"And?" Lady Cresswood prompted.

"I found a note bearing what I can only presume to be her name, Miss Mary Hamilton, M and H like on the brushes. There was a street address as well, but, alas, there was no town given."

Lord Cresswood heard no more. He let the murmur of conversation wash over him as he realized with abhorrence that the woman above stairs matched Sir Peter's description of his lightskirt exactly, even to her very name. Was it possible that he was housing a fraudulent, scheming female?

Three

The fire in the library burned low as Charles sat pondering the dilemma of Miss Mary Hamilton. A letter to Sir Peter was on its way to London even now, urging him to come to Oakhill at once. Only his friend could confirm if this woman was the young siren from London who'd fleeced the baronet out of five hundred pounds.

What if he was wrong about the woman? After all, he reasoned, the name Mary was very popular and he personally knew several Hamiltons who were not related. Still, her circumstances of being unescorted were damning for one who aspired to gentility. Had the so-called brother taken the money and abandoned her to her own devices? For some reason, the thought that she was a common bit of muslin caused a tightness in his stomach. Such a waste.

A knock on the door startled him, since all the family were now abed. "Enter."

The upstairs maid, Sally, came rather hesitantly through the door. "My lord, I didn't know if I should disturb you, but the young miss is finally awake and all. Mrs. Warren wanted to be told at once, but it being so late I didn't want to bother the lady."

Charles rose, relishing the opportunity to speak privately with his mysterious visitor. "I shall go to Miss Hamilton. Go to the kitchen and see if there is any soup left from dinner, for I am certain she is famished."

The servant had barely left when Charles strode from the room and up the stairs. He wanted to speak with the woman at once. He would have the truth even if he had to bluff her into admitting it. Unlike Peter, he would not fall prey to a pair of blue eyes and golden blond hair. His concern had been only for her well-being. He would send this swindler on her way as quickly as possible.

He knew it was improper for a gentleman to be in the girl's room alone, but this conversation would demand privacy. It was likely the baggage wasn't even truly a lady.

By the time he reached the door to the Blue Room, the earl was convinced that he was on a mission to protect his sister and mother from exposure to a wanton who used her wiles to get money from gentlemen. Without so much as knocking, he entered the room.

He closed the door quietly, then turned to observe his unwanted guest. A lone branch of candles sat on a table beside the large bed where the woman rested.

Miss Hamilton lay with closed eyes, unaware of his presence. The light from the candles bathed the young woman in a soft golden glow. He watched her silently for several minutes.

Charles was surprised to find the girl more beautiful than he remembered. Golden hair flowed from beneath a lacy night cap, lying in a mass of curls about her shoulders. Long dark lashes rested upon the porcelain cheeks of a delicately carved face. A blue dressing gown, which he thought belonged to his mother, gave her a look of sweet, feminine vulnerability. He was suddenly struck with an overwhelming urge to comfort her.

Stepping forward, the earl was about to touch her cheek when his gaze was drawn to the glitter of the silver brushes lying on the bedside table. The M and H etched into the back reminded him this creature might well be Sir Peter's Mary Hamilton. His back stiffened as he regained his resolve to have the woman gone from Oakhill. He drew his hand back to his side. "Miss Hamilton."

The young woman's eyes opened with a start. They seemed to be full of fear and confusion when she gazed at him. She nervously clutched at the covers, pulling them to her chin in a protective gesture. Slowly the fear left her gaze, replaced with one of questioning as she became aware of her surroundings.

"I apologize for startling you. I am Lord Cresswood." He was surprised at how cold and gruff his voice sounded.

Giving him a puzzled look, she answered, "Yes, my lord, I believe you introduced yourself when your brother brought me into your home. I wish to say how much I appreciate all that you and your family have done for me. I know——"

"Miss Hamilton, we have done for you what we would do for any stranger who was injured by a member of this family. Please do not dwell upon the matter," he brusquely interrupted her, amazed at how soft and gentle her voice was.

"Very well, my lord, as you wish," Miranda answered, falling silent in the face of his rudeness. She was puzzled by his attitude. It was almost as if he already knew she was Sylvester's stepsister. But that wasn't possible, for he was calling her by her old governess's name.

Cresswood found it difficult to look at the beguiling face while he spoke. He walked to a window. Drawing back the drapes, he looked out into the moonlit night, giving himself time to gather his thoughts. No matter if she were the cheapest ladybird in the city, his family owed her an acceptable convalescence due to his brother's negligence. They couldn't shirk their duty, no matter the circumstances.

Still, he wanted to know if his suspicions were true. Dropping the drape, he asked, "Was there someone you wanted us to inform about your whereabouts? Parents or a sister or brother?" He'd stressed the last word despite his best intentions.

"My lord?" she asked hesitantly, clutching the covers nervously. He thought she paled a bit.

"Did you wish us to inform someone of your accident?"

The girl gazed at him, making no comment. She seemed unable to respond to the simple question. Her hand came up to tug at a ribbon on her dressing gown. At last, she spoke barely above a whisper. "There is no one, sir. No one was expecting me."

The earl was filled with a vague sense of sadness at the sound of loneliness in her voice. No one that beautiful should be adrift in the world alone. Then he mentally chided himself. He was allowing his good judgment to be overwhelmed by sympathy for a female who might well be just a common, scheming jade.

The door opened and Sally entered carrying a tray with a small bowl of soup and a pot of tea. Realizing the injured woman needed nourishment and he would likely get nothing further from her tonight, Cresswood bowed farewell. "I shall leave you to your meal. We shall speak further in the morning. Good night, Miss Hamilton."

Without looking back, he left the chamber. Standing in the hallway in front of her room, Cresswood berated himself for his weakness. If she was Sir Peter's lightskirt, she was very good. If she wasn't . . . his thoughts trailed off. All he could think of was how fragile she'd looked lying in the large bed. Cursing at the unresolved outcome of the interview, he strode to his room to retire, but would he get any sleep?

Inside the bedchamber, Miranda listened to his footsteps recede. Lord Cresswood hadn't been exactly rude, but there was something in his manner that disturbed her. He was suspicious of her circumstances, no doubt. Or had he been merely scandalized by her traveling alone on the road?

"Here you are, Miss. Starved you must be." The maid sat the tray on Miranda's lap, and the fragrant smell of turtle soup drove all thoughts of the earl from Miranda's mind. She'd been two days without a meal and her worries would have to wait.

The following morning Miranda opened her eyes to bright sunlight.

Memory of the earl's visit flooded her immediately. She hadn't expected him to come last night. The young maid who'd sat with her said she would bring Mrs. Warren, but instead she'd been faced with a strangely hostile host. Miranda turned over to find an older maid now sitting in Sally's chair.

"Good morning," Miranda greeted the servant.

The woman looked up from her darning. Unlike the cheerful Sally, this maid stared intently. "Lady Cresswood sent for Dr. Mason. She herself will be here to visit you soon." The maid continued to gaze at her with eyes full of suspicion.

Her close scrutiny reminded Miranda that, except for a false name, she was unknown to the Bentons. They would want an explanation about why she was traveling unaccompanied and on foot. While she pondered what to tell them, a knock on the door interrupted her thoughts. She bade the visitor to enter.

With a flutter of cherry silk ribbons trimming a grey muslin gown, Mrs. Warren arrived. She was accompanied by a regal woman somewhat older, but clad elegantly in blue silk. Her air and proud carriage alerted Miranda that she was meeting her hostess.

The lady smiled at Miranda. "Good morning, Miss Hamilton. I am Lucilla, Dowager Countess of Cresswood. May I bid you welcome to Oakhill Manor and tell you how sorry I am about your unfortunate accident? My younger son wishes me to request a meeting with you to apologize to you in person for his reckless driving."

Miranda could only vaguely remember the young man who'd run her down. "Please don't blame your son for hitting someone who was foolish enough to cross near a curve. I should very much like to apologize to the gentleman for endangering his team."

"Very prettily said, Miss Hamilton, but Julian's carriage mishaps are too frequent to ignore completely. I assure you, he was scolded and I think he will be more careful in the future." Lady Cresswood took a seat near the bed. "But tell me, my dear, is there someone we should notify about your accident?"

Miranda hesitated at the question. Last night it had seemed a simple thing to deceive the Bentons about her identity. This morning, looking into the kind eyes of Lady Cresswood and Mrs. Warren, it was not so easy. But even as she saw the compassion on the faces of the two women, she thought about Sylvester and his plot. Her fear of him made her continue with her plan. She would keep as close to the truth as possible. "I am an orphan, Lady Cresswood. My father died when I was nine and my mother two years ago. Since then I have been living in a small village near Brighton. I was making my way to London to apply for a position as a governess when a carriage accident stranded me. Unfortunately, my trunks were sent ahead and await me at the Bull and Mouth. You have no need to worry about someone looking for me."

Someone tapped at the door as Lady Cresswood was about to speak. A dark-haired girl and young man entered the room at the dowager's command. Miranda recognized the earl's brother and thought him to be near her age, while his sister looked some years younger. With their raven hair and grey eyes one would know they were related even in a crowded room. Eyes very similar in colour, but far kinder than the pair that had stared so coldly at her last night.

The girl smiled at Miranda. "I heard you were awake. I am Lady Ellen Benton. We are delighted to have you at Oakhill, although I hope you will forgive my brother for the manner in which he forced you to visit. This is Julian." She gestured at the young man, who gazed uncomfortably at Miranda. "He is truly a likable fellow, when he is not behind his team." Lady Ellen's grey eyes twinkled as she came near the bed.

The young man glared at his sister before he stepped near the bed with great dignity. "Miss Hamilton, I pray you will believe I am grievously sorry for having injured you, and hope you will accept my deepest apologies."

Miranda smiled at the embarrassed young man to ease his chagrin. "Thank you, but 'tis I who must apologize to you, sir. Did your team come to any harm?"

Julian's face registered surprise. "No, the horses are in fine fettle. I would like to show them to you and prove I can be trusted with the ribbons, if you will allow me to drive out with you when you are better. I fear you will become quite bored staying in this room, for I did when I broke my arm last year."

"I would very much enjoy an outing when I am feeling better. Thank you, sir." Miranda liked the open sincerity in the young lord's face.

Eyes bright with merriment, Lady Cresswood sat back as she gazed lovingly at her youngest son. "Well, Julian, before you impress Miss Hamilton with your driving skills, it might be preferable, at least for the present, to find a quieter form of entertainment—a book of verse, or a novel from the library."

Julian was eager to be of help to the young lady. "Yes, that would be just the thing. Do you have a preference, Miss Hamilton?"

"I must confess to a fondness for novels. It is a terrible failing, I admit, but I usually find poetry quite melancholy."

"Well, my dear, if it's a failing, I fear I, too, suffer from it," Lady Cresswood confessed. "Julian, I believe I have a book she would enjoy. It is still beside my bed." She turned to the older maid. "Please fetch it for her. That should keep you entertained for now, my dear. Later, Julian can look through the library and find another selection for you."

Lady Cresswood smiled at her daughter. "Will you go and see if Dr. Mason has arrived yet, my dear?"

"I heard a commotion in the front hall when Julian and I came up. I shall go for now, but if the doctor approves, I shall sit with you this afternoon, Miss Hamilton." Ellen took her brother's arm, tugging gently to get him to leave, because he stood gazing distractedly at the patient.

"That would be delightful, Lady Ellen, but I cannot promise I shall stay awake. I have difficulty keeping my eyes open just yet."

"We don't want to tire our guest, Ellen. You may visit her again tomorrow. Now, go see if you can find Dr. Mason. I am sure our patient would very much like her breakfast and that must wait until the doctor is finished." Lady Cresswood stood, then looked back at Miranda. "As soon as he leaves, Cook will send up something to tempt your appetite."

Miranda smiled shyly. "Thank you, Lady Cresswood. That would be most welcome."

Lord Cresswood reined in his gelding at the top of a small rise facing Oakhill. The manor looked peaceful in the early morning mist. His black horse shifted restlessly under him, responding to his rider's tension. Despite riding since seven o'clock that morning, the earl still wrestled with the dilemma of his unwanted guest.

Before leaving the manor, he had learned that the messenger sent to fetch Sir Peter had not returned. Where could his old friend be?

Unfortunately, the morning ride round the estate hadn't cleared his thoughts in the least. Without Sir Peter, he must determine in his own mind if their guest was the same Mary Hamilton that the baronet knew. His conversation with her last night had confirmed nothing.

He had to decide how to handle Miss Hamilton. If she *was* Sir Peter's swindler, he wanted her out of the house as soon as she was able to travel. He did not want his mother or sister exposed to such common baggage. What worried him most was that his naive brother might succumb to the wiles of the beautiful young temptress.

But what if she wasn't the guilty lady? Then his family had an obligation not only to care for her until she recovered, but to make certain she reached her final destination safely. Cynically, he wondered what the likelihood was of her being innocent.

The chiming of the church bell in the village made him realize the lateness of the hour. With a light touch, he turned his horse toward the stables. He knew he must take some action to get this woman out of the house as quickly as possible if she were the swindler, even if he must personally drive her all the way to London. All would be clear as soon as Peter arrived.

As he came up the drive, Cresswood saw Dr. Mason's carriage sitting in the stable yard. The earl jumped down, leaving his horse with a young groom who came forward for the reins, and walked around the house to the front and entered through the Great Hall. As he strode into the Green Drawing Room, he found Julian reading the *Morning Post*.

"What has Dr. Mason to say?" Cresswood asked his brother abruptly as he drew off his York tan gloves.

"Miss Hamilton is awake, Charles, and appears to be fine. Of course, that is only Cousin Amelia's opinion, but Mother is hopeful as well. Is it not wonderful news?" Julian smiled happily as he shared the information.

"Yes, very good news." Charles thought it best to not mention his nocturnal visit to the woman's room. "Is Mother with the doctor now?"

"Yes, but they should be down anytime now. Mason arrived over thirty minutes ago." Julian folded the paper and placed it on the table. His gaze followed his brother as that gentleman paced back and forth. "The best news is that I got an opportunity to apologize to Miss Hamilton and she was most gracious. She tried to shoulder some of the blame for crossing on a curve. She appears to be a very reasonable young lady." Julian wondered about his brother's strange restlessness. "You seem agitated, Charles. Is there some problem with the estate?"

"No, I only want this matter resolved as quickly as possible. You need to get back to your studies and I want to return to London." Cresswood looked at his brother's innocent face and knew he did not want the boy involved any further with this mysterious woman.

Julian's back stiffened. "You have no need to remain if you have business elsewhere. *I* can handle this matter, and will, gladly, since I am the one responsible for Miss

Hamilton's accident." He rose and marched from the room, every line of his body stiff with anger.

Cresswood stood for several minutes, realizing he'd been too abrupt with Julian. He was about to follow his brother to soothe the boy's injured pride, when his mother entered the drawing room, trailed by the family physician. "There you are, Charles. Dr. Mason has such wonderful news for us about Miss Hamilton."

Cresswood eyed the doctor hopefully. The old man waited while the dowager countess took a seat, then sat opposite on the sofa. "Would you care for something to drink, Doctor?" Cresswood asked politely.

"I took the liberty of ordering tea." The dowager smiled at the old family doctor. "I was sure it would be most welcomed on such a cold morning."

"It would indeed, Lady Cresswood. However, I should only remain a few minutes. Lady Hobson's baby is on the way and I must get to Wheaton Hall before the first Hobson heir makes an appearance. You know how worried first-time fathers can be, and the baron is no different," Mason said. Lady Cresswood nodded in agreement.

"Doctor, can you tell us when Miss Hamilton will be ready to travel?" Cresswood asked impatiently. He had no time for pleasantries this morning.

"I think you may be getting a little ahead of things, speaking of traveling so soon, your lordship," the physician warned the earl. "The patient is awake, but I think you should plan on caring for the young lady for at least a fortnight. A head injury such as she has sustained can be quite serious. There is also the matter of the injury to her limb. While it is not serious, it will be very painful when she begins to walk."

Charles felt like a ton of bricks had just fallen on him. No matter who the lady was, she deserved and needed their assistance to her recovery. He would have to put his mind to a plan for keeping his family away from the guest until Peter came. Where the devil could he be?

Lady Cresswood frowned at her son before turning to the doctor. "There is no rush for Miss Hamilton to leave, Dr. Mason. My son is only worried that her relatives will be most concerned about her whereabouts. But she assures me no one is expecting her arrival. The poor girl is an orphan. We will gladly take care of her until she is ready to continue her journey." The dowager smiled. "Why, I think I shall ask her to remain with us through the coming holidays."

Charles opened his mouth to protest, then stayed his speech. He would know something long before the Yule season. Once he had proof, Miss Hamilton would be on her way.

Watching his mother while she directed Miller to serve the doctor tea, he could tell that she was distressed with his show of bad manners by the tiny crease appearing between her brows. His desire to get the girl out of the house had affected his judgment, and the last thing he wanted was to upset his mother. He must learn to be patient. Peter would be here soon and all his questions would be at an end.

There was a round of small talk about the neighborhood as they drank their tea, during which the earl made a special effort to appease his mother's sensibilities. After scarcely ten minutes, Dr. Mason put down his tea cup and rose to leave. Lord Cresswood stood immediately to escort the physician to the front hallway. He said all that was proper, but his mind was already at work on finding a plan to keep his family from spending too much time with the unknown lady upstairs.

Returning to the drawing room, he was anxious to learn what his parent knew. "Mother, what did this . . . woman tell you about herself?"

Lady Cresswood knew her son well. There could be no kinder heart in the world, but he too often jumped to the wrong conclusion on the flimsiest of evidence, like with Julian and the carriage accident. Unfortunately, once his mind was set on a course it was difficult to sway him. "Charles, I am not sure what odd idea you have developed about Miss Hamilton, but she seems to be of genteel birth. I don't know any of the details, save that she is an orphan who has been living near Brighton. A carriage accident left her stranded and that was the reason she was on the road with so few of her belongings."

"Mother, you know practically nothing about this young woman and you know even less about the darker side of Society. You must not think her to be a lady of Quality merely because she dresses or speaks properly. I would suggest you and Ellen avoid socializing with someone whose background is such a mystery."

His mother shook her head in disappointment. "Charles, there are many things about which you have a greater knowledge than I. However, I think I am quite capable of telling when someone is gently bred. You are very much mistaken if you think her present circumstances are the key to Miss Hamilton. There is one thing

I am sure of. Breeding always shows." With those words, she rose and left her son in the parlor.

Watching his mother depart, Cresswood realized she might be right, for he had little proof of his suspicions. He could be drawing all the wrong conclusions, but he doubted it. Striding toward the stairway, he decided to put the matter from his mind for the time being. Still, he was surprised at how low his spirits were at the thought of having to remove this young woman from his home. What was the matter with him? It was as if she had the ability to steal his will.

Stiffening his back, he concluded he could not allow anything or anyone to weaken his resolution to learn the truth. Then he went to change out of his riding clothes. Hopefully Sir Peter would be at Oakhill by nightfall and end his quandary.

Four

Some thirty minutes later, dressed suitably for the morning in black coat, light grey-striped waistcoat and grey pantaloons, the earl headed downstairs to look for someone to help lift his black mood. He needed companionship to get the girl's lovely face from his mind.

Ellen, just returning from outdoors, was directing her maid to take a parcel to Mrs. Warren when Cresswood came down the stairs. Looking up, she called out, "There you are, Charles." She allowed the footman to remove her fur-lined mantle before continuing. "We've just returned from the village on an errand for Cousin Amelia. Will you join me for a cup of tea? I fear I am chilled to the bone after that jaunt to the chemist."

"I shall sit with you while you have your tea, but why did you not have Julian or Reggie drive you to the village?" Cresswood asked, pleased to see her. He knew his young sister could brighten his mood. "I am certain our cousin would have been delighted to display his new carriage. I believe he lives to be admired."

Laughing, Ellen responded, "So he does, but admired in the afternoon. He rarely puts in an appearance before then. As for Julian, I believe he is off somewhere finding books to keep Miss Hamilton occupied during her convalescence." Seeing Charles's frown, she added, "I think it is his way of doing penance for injuring her. When we visited her this morning, she expressed a desire for something to read."

Looking thoughtfully at Ellen, the earl realized she'd just given him a wonderful idea. "Yes, that is what the young lady needs. I would suggest you and Julian give her as much time to rest as possible. It very likely might slow her recovery to have a steady stream of visitors."

"Well, dear brother, are you planning on replacing Dr. Mason as her physician? He gave us the same advice this morning. Cousin Amelia has made it her duty to make sure we follow his instructions to the letter. She has been quite wonderful with Miss Hamilton. Now, while I enjoy talking with you, I am very much chilled. Perhaps we might find a nice warm fire."

Taking his sister's arm, he led her across the hall. "Please accept my apology for keeping you standing. My manners have been sadly lacking since I returned to Oakhill. I believe the library will do nicely. Come and tell me what amusements you have had since I last visited the manor."

"Only if you take me riding in the morning. I shall forgive your shocking neglect today, for I know you have estate business to handle and the house is a bit topsy-turvy with an injured guest. I must own I had quite forgotten we were to ride this morning myself, what with the good news from the patient's room. But I would dearly love a good gallop tomorrow."

"Then I promise to be at the stables by eight o'clock with horses ready. Mayhap Julian would care to join us." Anything to get the boy out of the house.

"Yes, it would be wonderful to have the three of us riding again like old times."

Laughing, the earl opened the door of the library and allowed his sister to enter. "Little one, what can you know of old times at the tender age of fifteen? When you are an old married lady, then we shall speak of old times. Now ring the bell for tea, while I move a chair closer to the fire."

Miranda lay in the warm comfort of the bed, alone with her thoughts while the maid returned her tray to the kitchen. Her mind drifted back to the meeting with the earl the night before. She tried to understand his coolness. He hadn't said as much, but clearly he wanted her gone. But could she blame him? In his eyes, she was a nobody who'd been wandering alone on the road. He'd been forced to accept her into his home and expose his sister and mother to who knew what manner of creature. Short of telling him her real identity, all she could do to relieve his hostility was to behave with the proper decorum and manners to show him she was a lady.

As Miranda turned to her side, a twinge of pain in her newly bound ankle reminded her she could not leave Oakhill as yet. She needed time to recover. But would the earl give her enough time? How could she convince Lord Cresswood to allow a complete stranger a fortnight under his roof? A stranger who had blackened her own character by her improper behavior of wandering the roads unaccompanied.

A knock interrupted her thoughts, and the door

opened to admit Mrs. Warren. "Are you feeling better for having eaten breakfast, my dear?"

"Yes, thank you, Mrs. Warren. I fear I was unable to do Cook's efforts justice, however," Miranda responded.

"Don't worry, Miss Hamilton. Your appetite will return with your strength. Now, I want you to promise you shan't let anyone disturb you today. The doctor wants you to get as much sleep as possible. I have ordered the family and the servants to let you rest. I shall visit you throughout the day should you need anything. Tomorrow will be time enough for having visitors."

"Will you stay and speak with me for a moment, Mrs. Warren? I know you must be quite busy, but I would appreciate company until I get sleepy."

With a pleased smile, Amelia Warren assented. She settled her thin frame in the chair beside the bed. "Please call me Cousin Amelia. Everyone does."

"Thank you, I would be honoured. And you may call me . . . Mary." Miranda hesitated over the false name. "How long have you been living at Oakhill Manor?"

As Amelia Warren began to tell the story of her life, Miranda realized that the older woman might be able to give her some understanding as to what kind of man the earl truly was.

At the conclusion of Cousin Amelia's tale, Miranda probed, "The earl and his family seem very nice." She hoped that would lead to the information she needed.

"My dear, I cannot tell you how positively wonderful my cousin's family is. They have all welcomed me as if I had grown up at Oakhill," Cousin Amelia said.

"The members of the family were all most welcoming

and friendly, but the earl seemed different. He seemed rather . . . reserved."

"You have met Cresswood?"

"Last evening, when I first awoke. Sally brought him. He seemed displeased with me in some way."

Cousin Amelia laughed. "Not with you child, surely. I would imagine Julian is more likely the cause for his behavior. It seems to take little to bring the two of them to words these days, what with Julian falling into one scrape or another. As for the earl, he is well liked by his staff and tenants. So you needn't worry about his mood, for he would be very kind to an injured traveler like yourself."

Miranda very much doubted Cousin Amelia's assertion that the earl was upset with Julian, but there was no need to voice her thoughts. As Cousin Amelia finished speaking, Miranda realized that she truly was very tired. "Yes, you are most likely correct. Thank you for taking time to talk with me, but I am beginning to feel fatigued."

"Excellent, my dear. I enjoyed our chat, but you need your rest." Cousin Amelia rose and picked up a book which lay on Miranda's bed. Putting it on the night table, she said, "You take a nap and I will visit you again."

Miranda sank into a light sleep, too tired to worry about her fate. The face of the earl came to her, telling her she must be gone from his estate. She tossed and turned in her restless slumber. As he spoke, she heard the sound of pounding hooves. In her dream, Sylvester arrived at the manor to take her home. Her stepbrother's face floated up in the blackness, bragging, "I have you now." She awoke with a start.

The shadows in the room had grown long. Miranda realized she'd slept away most of the afternoon. She was surprisingly hungry and wondered when someone would visit her.

Turning over in bed, she looked at the glowing embers in the fireplace and pondered how to handle the earl. She longed to see his face as she remembered it from her first meeting, full of concern. But the haughty, cold look of last night was all he was likely to show her while she remained at Oakhill.

She sighed as she reflected on her deception of the Bentons. It went against her nature to be dishonest, but she knew she must continue her role if she were to escape the detestable marriage Sylvester had arranged.

The door opened as she lay in the darkening room. " 'Twas your job to make sure Miss Hamilton's fire didn't go out," the maid called Sally said. "I know 'tis difficult, but until Miss is better, no footman should do it. You had no good reason for hovering around the kitchen just to watch them two go at one another."

The pair moved quietly towards the fireplace as Miranda watched. She could see the second person was a large older maid, dressed in an unusually dirty apron and carrying a coal scuttle. The woman responded softly, "Sal, you know when that bag of wind Gresham and Lord Julian's man get around each other there is always a good turn-up. I thought Hawkins was goin' to plant a facer on old Gresham when he suggested that Lord Julian only kept Ruby around to annoy Mr. Chartley and that the earl ought to get rid of her."

" 'Tis a shame Lord Julian brought Ruby to the manor and let her get near Mr. Chartley's boots. But Gresham has rocks in his head if he thinks his lordship will order Lord Julian to get rid of her, for a kinder-hearted man I never knew than the earl." Sally reached the fireplace and began to light candles on the mantel as the second maid poured the coals on the dying fire.

Miranda decided to let the pair know she was awake. "Good evening, Sally. I take it there has been trouble below stairs."

Two startled faces turned towards Miranda. Sally curtsied. "Miss Hamilton, I apologize if we wakened you. This here is Maggie and she was supposed to keep your fire goin' so the room wouldn't get chilled. I'm afraid she got distracted and now the fire has almost gone out."

Miranda smiled at the large maid. "Don't worry, Maggie, I have been sleeping here comfortably and didn't need a fire. Now I must apologize for eavesdropping, but who is Ruby? I thought I had met all the members of the family."

Maggie laughed. "Well, Ruby is Lord Julian's dog and she be a lovable red mongrel, but she can make some mischief if she be left by herself in the house. Myself, I don't reckon it was her what scratched them boots, but old Gresham be rantin' and a-ravin' about it like them boots was completely ruint."

"And do you think Lord Cresswood will do anything bad to Ruby?" Miranda asked with interest as Maggie stoked the embers with an iron.

"No, Miss, he'll probably order Ruby to be kept at the stables until their cousin leaves and make Lord Julian pay for a new pair of boots should that be what Mr. Chartley wants. Not but what that young man's pockets are quite full of blunt and he don't need anyone buyin' him anythin'." Sally came over to light several candles by the bed.

As the two worked at their jobs, a knock came at the door and Cousin Amelia entered. "Have you been able to get any sleep, my dear?" Mrs. Warren asked, frowning at the two servants who were in the room.

"Yes, thank you. I was lying here awake when Sally and Maggie came in quietly to restoke the fire and light the candles. I must confess to distracting them by asking questions about the mysterious Ruby."

"Ruby!" Mrs. Warren's eyes grew round as her gaze darted anxiously about the room. "That dog has not gotten in here as well, has she? I have never been able to understand why anyone would want such a dirty pet. Full of diseases they are."

Miranda hesitated to tell Amelia she had a fondness for dogs as well. She merely replied, "As an only child, I found my dog to be good company." Sylvester had been quite grown when her mother had married the late Lord Redford, so Miranda never thought of him as a relation.

Cousin Amelia nodded. "An only child, how sad. It is very difficult to have no family after your parents are gone. I was lucky enough to have cousins, but what about you, my dear? Do you have anyone to stay with after you reach London?"

Miranda tugged nervously at the blanket over her. She knew this was a dangerous area. "I planned to apply for a position as governess that is coming open in the spring. A dear friend of mine had written to tell me about it."

"Did you want us to notify her of your accident?" Amelia looked hopeful.

"No, thank you," Miranda answered hurriedly. "She was not expecting me to come so soon to apply for the position. I had thought to surprise her."

"Well, my dear, if you change your mind, simply tell one of the maids and they can furnish you with pen and paper to write anyone you wish. Now, I know that you must be starving after your long nap. Would you like a light tea before dinner?"

Relieved the subject of sending a message to someone was dropped, Miranda responded, "Yes, I would enjoy that immensely. Won't you join me?"

"I would be delighted," the elder woman accepted. "Sally, inform her ladyship that I shall be absent from the family tea."

The rest of the evening passed quickly for Miranda. She had little time to think about the problem of the earl's cool behavior. Cousin Amelia agreed to allow several visitors to see how Miranda was doing, after she assured her nurse that she wasn't the least bit sleepy.

Julian arrived, bearing several new books he'd found in the library and promising her he would continue to look for more. He was quickly shooed away by his cousin. Ellen soon appeared, looking quite pretty in yellow, to chatter away for the few minutes she was allowed. Miranda was surprised at how much she liked the young pair and knew she would have enjoyed getting to know them if only time and circumstances permitted.

The next visitors for the evening were Lord Cresswood, dressed elegantly in a black coat with gleaming white waistcoat, and his mother, in a fashionable green silk evening gown. Miranda's heart pounded as she gazed up at the earl's handsome face.

"Good evening, Miss Hamilton. My mother and I wished to see how you progress."

His tone was distant, formal yet polite. Nothing to encourage Miranda that he'd changed his thoughts on wanting a strange woman gone from his home.

"G-Good evening, my lord, Lady Cresswood. I am much improved from this morning."

The dowager, ever friendly, stepped to the bed, covering Miranda's hand with her own. She did not see the slight frown on her son's face—but Miranda did.

"That is wonderful news, is it not, Charles?" The lady continued to speak without waiting for her son's reply. "I am pleased to say you have more colour in your cheeks than when I saw you last."

"I am truly feeling stronger. My head has not ached since this morning," Miranda responded to her kind hostess, ignoring the dark looks from the earl. She was beginning to feel annoyed with the gentleman's behavior towards her. After all, she was Lady Miranda Henley, daughter of the late Earl of Manville, and while he didn't know it, she hadn't behaved in any improper manner in his household. How dare he still treat her like some low woman!

The dowager countess took a seat. "I was thinking about your being from near Brighton. Are you any relation to Sir Howard Hamilton? He was an old friend of my husband, the late earl."

All Miranda's anger at the earl fled as the subject of her ancestry was discussed. Stuttering out her answers she said, "N-no, I-I am sure there are many different branches of the Hamilton family."

Lady Cresswood's hazel gaze rested on Miranda as

she fidgeted with the quilt. She could feel the earl's steady scrutiny, as if he was trying to pierce her very soul. Both mother and son seemed to be waiting for their guest to volunteer information about her family background.

Remembering her governess's true history, Miranda borrowed that. "My father was a vicar in a small parish near Exeter. All of his family came from Devon."

"Ah, then I would not be familiar with them, for I have never been to Devon," Lady Cresswood said. "And your mother? What was her maiden name? It would be delightful if I truly did know one of your relatives."

Feeling more uncomfortable, and not knowing what Missy's mother's name had been, Miranda used her real mother's name. "My mother was a Camden before she married."

"Camden," Lady Cresswood said slowly. "Camden. Why, I went to school with an Olivia Camden. She had such a sweet nature. I liked her very much. Could she . . . no, she married a young lord who lived near Plymouth. What was his name? Oh, I remember! she married William Henley, fourth Earl of Manville—or was it fifth? He was an excellent fellow. All the girls had eyes for him, but Olivia won his heart."

Miranda's throat tightened with tears as she realized the dowager countess was speaking of her own dear mother and father. She longed to break her silence, to share fond memories of her beloved parents. But as the earl stood there so cold and alert, she had no way of knowing what Sylvester might have said about his reason for being at the Grey Swan that day. Had he spoken of looking for his missing relative? Miranda wouldn't take a chance.

Lady Cresswood rose with a sigh. "I know it was gooseish to think I would know your family, but sometimes it seems such a small world. We must be going, or the gong will sound before we can reach the drawing room." Lady Cresswood walked to the door. The earl hesitated a moment as if he were going to say something else. His grey eyes were unreadable as they observed Miranda. Then he quietly wished her a good night.

As the door closed behind the pair, Miranda took a deep breath. It had been difficult to resist telling Lady Cresswood and her son the truth. It would have been a very silly thing to do knowing that Sylvester still searched for her and that the earl, no doubt, was looking for any excuse to have her gone from under his roof. She longed to tell the Bentons everything, but she would just have to put that thought out of her mind.

Later, after her supper dishes were cleared away, Miranda wondered if Amelia was right. Had the earl merely been distracted by his anger at Lord Julian? There had been less overt hostility in him at this meeting. She would have to see how he behaved on the morrow. Surely by now Sylvester had gone on to London. 'Twas likely she hadn't much to fear as long as she continued being Mary Hamilton. With that comforting thought, she drifted into a peaceful sleep.

Five

The following morning Lord Cresswood rose early, but found his messenger still hadn't returned with news from his friend, Sir Peter. He'd told the fellow to go all the way to Weldon Park in Northumberland if the baronet was not in Town. Since the servant hadn't returned, it was clear that was where he'd gone.

Disappointed, Charles sat down and read the social column of the *Morning Post,* hoping to see news of the gentleman, but there was no mention of the baronet. While perusing the rest of the paper, he spied a notice that gave him a plan for keeping his younger siblings occupied and away from their unwanted visitor's room. He felt certain by the evening Sir Peter would arrive at Oakhill.

At breakfast, he announced he wanted to inspect a horse that Lord Newbury had for sale and inquired if anyone would be interested in going along to Lewes. As he'd suspected, both his brother and sister were eager to accompany him, but they worried about leaving their mother and cousin to tend their injured guest unassisted. Assuring them they were doing Miss Hamilton a favor by allowing her to rest, he convinced the pair to join him.

They attempted to rouse Reggie, but that young man declined through his servant, saying he might inspect the shops in Crawley instead. Charles suspected more likely he wanted to be seen in all his splendor by the locals.

The trio informed their mother of their plans, then set out for Newbury Hall on horseback.

Arriving back at six that evening, all had to rush to be dressed by seven. Charles was disappointed to learn that Sir Peter still hadn't arrived or sent a message. What could be keeping him?

The family members sat in the drawing room having tea after dinner, while Ellen rhapsodized about the new horse her brother had purchased. In the middle of her discourse, she halted and inquired about Miss Hamilton.

Cousin Amelia seemed pleased to have all eyes on her. "The doctor wants her to get up and start moving about soon. 'Tis never good to leave an ankle injury go too long before one uses it. It might get terribly stiff."

Charles dreaded the thought of the woman being in company with his family as long as her history remained unknown. "Miss Hamilton would do well to remain in her room for a while yet. She might fall on the stairs if she were to try to come to the drawing room."

Reginald, dressed in a stunning plum coat with a green and white striped waistcoat, joined the conversation. "Who is this M-Miss Hamilton you keep speaking of?"

With a slight flush of embarrassment, Julian, who sat next to Ellen, answered, "Miss Hamilton is the young lady whom I injured while driving down to Oakhill several days ago."

"Why is Charles wanting her to be left alone in her

room? Don't seem quite the thing to ignore one's guest. Bad *ton,*" Reginald informed the family.

"Oh, you very much mistake the case, Mr. Chartley." Cousin Amelia rushed to the earl's defense. "Miss Hamilton is unable to leave her room due to her injuries. Lord Cresswood would never treat a guest with such a shocking lack of manners. He is most concerned with Miss Hamilton's well being."

Cresswood stood uncomfortably before the fireplace as Cousin Amelia smiled up at him. He was in a difficult situation, knowing more about what might be true of the young woman than the others. But he didn't wish to reveal the possibility of her tawdry past to his family. "I shall certainly be guided by Dr. Mason, but I suggest we not worry or tire Miss Hamilton with unnecessary visits or trips downstairs. The young woman told Mother about her plans. She must be fully recovered and on her way to Town before the end of next month."

Ellen argued against Cresswood's plan. "I always feel better when friends are around me during an illness. I am sure the doctor will want us to keep Mary amused when she is not resting."

The young dandy placed his cup upon a table and joined Cresswood by the fireplace. "I live for the latest on-dits of Society. Perhaps I should pay the young lady a visit to amuse her. M-Mama is delighted with m-my visits and forgets her ailments after I entertain her with stories of the royals and their flirts."

"You are acquainted with the royals?" Ellen gazed at her cousin with rounded eyes.

"Don't be such a country mouse, Ellen. Everyone who

is genteel rubs elbows with the Carlton House set in Society," Julian interjected with a bored air of sophistication.

"I was unaware you are acquainted with the Prince Regent, Julian." Cresswood was amused at his brother's jaded attitude.

Julian blushed slightly, but smiled at his brother's teasing. "Well, as to that, 'tis what I have heard."

Turning to his cousin, the earl continued his efforts to keep the family away from their mysterious guest. "Reggie, I very much doubt Miss Hamilton is interested in what Society's swells are doing, royal or otherwise. She is a . . . governess."

"I say, Julian, I should think a governess beneath your touch. M-Must be some dashedly pretty gals around Town to keep a lad like you entertained without m-making off with a governess." Reginald looked perplexed by his cousin's choice of traveling companion.

"Making off?" Julian uttered loudly, "I ran *over* Miss Hamilton, not *off* with her. What kind of muttonhead do you take me for?"

Reginald looked surprised by such a volatile outburst in the drawing room. He raised his quizzing glass to eye his young cousin disdainfully.

Julian looked sheepishly at his mother and apologized for his behavior. Casting a disgusted look at the dandy, Julian set down his empty cup and begged to be excused for the evening.

Walking his brother to the door, Cresswood quietly murmured, "You must forgive Reggie. He simply is not around here often enough to know the truth."

Puzzled, Julian asked, "What truth?"

"Why the truth about what kind of muttonhead you

are. Only your family knows that." Cresswood gave his brother a teasing grin.

Julian smiled with real amusement as his brother closed the door after him.

The fire burned low as Miranda snuggled tiredly under her covers. She felt better and hoped to soon be back on her feet.

A knock at the door startled her. She glanced at Sally, who sat by the fire. Miranda signaled the girl to remain seated and called for the visitor to enter.

The door opened stealthily to reveal Lord Julian Benton, looking boyishly handsome in evening clothes. "I hope I didn't wake you. I know I should not be here, but I wished to see you for a few moments before retiring to see how you are feeling. I knew Sally was staying with you one last night, so I am flouting the conventions only a trifle." The young man nodded to Sally as he entered, leaving the door fully open.

Miranda sensed a certain restlessness in Julian as he idly moved around the room. "I am much better, thank you. I hope you don't remain at home because of me."

Strolling up to the bed, he took a seat in the nearby chair. "No, I appreciate any excuse not to have to return to Oxford. I am ready to be done with books and dons. I simply wish I could persuade Charles to let me make my own decisions. He insists on still treating me like a child."

"And does he have cause?" Miranda questioned gently.

A look of guilt flashed across the young man's face. "Well, I would say I behaved rather badly last summer when Charles forbid me to speak anymore of joining the army." Sitting back in the chair, he rested his chin upon his hand. "I read the letters of my cousin, Daniel Turner, and he's told us of his adventures for so many years I longed to experience some excitement myself. After all, I am a younger son and need an occupation. What better place than the army?"

Miranda, hoping to help repay Lady Cresswood for her kindness, asked, "Why must your adventures be in the military? My father's brother was in the army. He often said being a soldier involved hours and hours of boredom topped with rare moments of absolute fear. He told me had I been a boy, he would have suggested another avocation."

Doubt clouded Julian eyes. "Perhaps he was not meant to be a soldier."

"Oh, no, he liked it very much. Stayed long enough to distinguish himself and attained the rank of general. He merely felt too many young men came in with the wrong idea about life in the army. You talk about adventure, but that is only one small part of being a soldier. There are the long marches in the rain, cold nights on the battlefield, and not seeing your loved ones for years on end. But my uncle said the worst was losing so many good friends during a fierce engagement." Miranda watched young Benton's melancholy face.

"I thought you were an orphan with no kin?" Julian asked as the mention of a relative struck him.

"My uncle died when I was fifteen. Some unknown malady took him while he was in India. I have no living relative in the world." Each time she thought she was past explaining her ancestry, another question arose, she thought in exasperation.

"Did my mother ask you to talk to me?" Julian narrowed his eyes suspiciously.

Miranda laughed. "No, I simply wanted to give you the advice I learned from him. You can ignore it if you like. I have never been very good at taking advice myself. I just remembered that I longed for adventure as a little girl after I heard some of my uncle's exciting stories. I would have my nurse take me to the harbor near my home and watch the ships come and go, always longing to be on one of them. I fear after my father died, my adventures were more unpleasant than wonderful. But enough about me. You should consider a different kind of adventure."

"What might that be?" Julian asked with tepid interest.

"Perhaps you might want to weigh the idea of traveling. I have read a great deal about how exciting it is in the West Indies and often thought I should like to travel down and visit the tropics myself. Sail with the trade winds and explore the islands, a new adventure on each one." Miranda's voice was full of longing yet enthusiastic.

Julian stood up as if captured by Miranda's excitement. He began to talk excitedly. "Yes, I had never thought of traveling there. Taking the Grand Tour is out of the question with Napoleon running loose. Do you think Cresswood might consider it?"

"Indeed, I cannot say, for I don't know your brother, but it is an alternative to the military and fraught with less danger. You must give it some thought, for Lord

Cresswood may be equally opposed to such a plan." Miranda stifled a yawn as she spoke.

"Miss Hamilton, you must think me devoid of all feelings, standing here chattering about my problems when you need your rest. My brother is forever saying we should not be up here pestering you. I promise to give your suggestion some careful thought," Julian said as he moved towards the door. "Good night. We shall speak further in the morning."

Miranda lay in bed wondering about the earl's strictures on his siblings to stay away from her. It very much confirmed her belief that he held her in some dislike. She was overwhelmed with depression.

Turning her thoughts to less daunting matters, she speculated about the wisdom of the idea she gave young Julian. She hoped Lady Cresswood would think it an equally good plan. But there could be no doubt the earl would dislike the idea because it had come from her.

Six

Lord Cresswood and Lady Ellen entered the manor through the front door the following morning. "That was exhilarating," she said, eyes twinkling. "I adore such gallops, and especially with you." The girl twirled around in the front hallway as she spoke, wisps of dark hair escaping her chignon, floating around her glowing face.

"I promise we shall go again before I leave." Cresswood smiled at Ellen. "You should get Julian to ride with you when he is home. I thought he came down quite often during the term."

"Yes, he is in and out. But there is usually some prize-fight or race he comes for. He cannot find time for his younger sister." Ellen removed her gloves and hat, handing them to the waiting Miller.

The clock in the hall chimed the hour. "Oh, my goodness, I must hurry and change. I promised Mama to take the baby bonnets Cousin Amelia made round to the vicar. He is taking them to the foundling home this afternoon." Standing on her toes, she kissed her brother's cheek, then rushed up the stairs.

Asking the butler his mother's direction, the earl joined her in the breakfast parlor. She appeared to be finishing her meal. "Good morning, Mother." He bent and kissed her cheek.

"Good morning, dearest. I was waiting for you. Won't you sit down and have a cup of tea? I wish to speak to you about Julian." His mother began to pour him a cup before he could protest he was still in his dirt from riding.

Seating himself with resignation, Charles asked, "What has Julian done this time?"

Giving a small sigh, Lady Cresswood retorted, "Must it always be something bad for me to wish to speak about your brother?"

"Of late it has appeared so. I must say if I am wrong, then I do apologize. 'Tis not to be supposed he decided to return to his studies?"

Laughter took away the dowager's frown. "No, indeed. That should be a miracle I don't expect I shall see in my lifetime. However, I had a most enlightening conversation with him just before you returned. He visited Miss Hamilton last evening. I shall make no mention of the impropriety of that. He said he wanted to see how she was recovering. I suspect he admires the young lady's courage." The dowager sipped her tea. "During the visit, she succeeded in directing his interest away from the idea of buying a pair of colours, if only for the time being. Although he has not mentioned such of late, you can have no doubt that he hasn't given up such a plan."

Leaning back in his chair, Cresswood folded his arms across his chest as he looked at his mother, his grey eyes becoming as flat and as unreadable as a stone. "And what might this new ambition be? To quit school and marry the unsuitable Miss Hamilton?" Rising, he began to pace round the table in agitation.

"Cresswood, you are being ridiculous. Julian has no interest in Miss Hamilton or any other young lady in a romantic way. He is mad for an adventure, not matrimony. What put such a preposterous idea in your head?"

The earl stopped his pacing in front of the windows and looked back at his mother with respect. A perceptive woman. He'd almost revealed what he suspected about Miss Hamilton. Returning to the table, he sat down with a ready response. "I fear it was Cousin Daniel's fault. We discussed Julian in Town last week and he said the boy should find a bride and settle down to get rid of this military nonsense." Seeing his mother's frown, he continued. "I told him Julian still needed some seasoning before he thought of marriage."

Doubt clouded Lady Cresswood's eyes. "I begin to think your attitude has more to do with Miss Hamilton and less with Julian. Cresswood, have you learned something about the young lady from your inquiries? You have behaved rather strangely towards her since she was brought here. Or . . . have *you* developed a *tendre* for her?"

"*Tendre!* Mother, I am not some green cub who falls for every pretty chit I see," Cresswood protested too strongly for his own comfort. In a quieter voice he continued, "No, I shall only say I have some suspicions about Miss Hamilton's background. Jamie has reported nothing from his inquiries."

"Suspicions? But you don't know anything for certain?" his mother asked skeptically.

"No, not for certain."

Rising, his mother walked over to the window and stood gazing out at the landscape. "I have come to believe there may be some mystery about Miss Hamilton. She seemed hesitant to speak of her family last evening." Pausing a moment, she turned to look at Cresswood. "But I believe it is not something unsavory and I feel to the bottom of my heart she is a lady of Quality. I could not be deceived for so long. Besides, after what she did last night, I feel we owe her a debt of gratitude."

Cynically raising an eyebrow, Cresswood asked, "What miracle has the lady wrought?"

"Julian came to me this morning talking about taking something like a Grand Tour."

Cresswood snorted. "Only the military is taking a tour of the Continent now. Julian knows that."

"He was not speaking of Europe. He referred to the West Indies. He suggested you might consider sending him with that young curate who is so bookish at the village church. Julian could continue his studies and see some of the world with a companion who would otherwise not get a chance to travel."

"I am sure Julian's motives in selecting a companion were very noble," Cresswood said dryly. More likely the boy was certain he could get his way with the shy curate.

Lady Cresswood ignored the earl's interruption. "He said Miss Hamilton pointed out what he longed for was adventure and it did not have to come in the army. He thought about it all night and came to realize she was right."

Charles sat quietly and thought about Miss Hamilton's suggestion. Putting his concerns about her aside, the plan had merit. He continued to idly stir his tea. After several minutes he looked back at his mother. "I shall have to give the idea some thought. 'Tis not something I intended for him to do."

Coming back to where Cresswood sat, his mother placed a loving hand upon his shoulder. "Julian needs a chance to spread his wings. 'Tis wrong to make him look to you for every decision. You had managed this family for almost two years by the time you were Julian's age. Give him the same opportunity to learn responsibility, at least for himself. I see no good coming of you two quarreling at nearly every meeting."

"In truth, there is very little quarreling. Julian simply flies into the boughs every time I try to tell him what my wishes for him are. I felt I needed to protect him, but I suppose he is getting old enough to run his own life," Cresswood said with dawning understanding. "I shall give the idea a fair chance. First, I must speak with the vicar and see if the curate is willing. Say nothing of the matter to Julian until all is settled."

"I shall not speak of it until I have your leave. Now, what about the matter of Miss Hamilton? Will you at least behave with civility until you know the truth of her situation? I believe we shall discover her to be the genteel lady she appears. I would very much dislike it should she be treated shabbily under this roof," his mother finished sternly.

The earl was surprised by her tone of voice. "As you wish, Mother." After all, he thought, Miss Hamilton would not get much opportunity to play any tricks if he kept his eye on her and kept Julian busy until the boy could be sent on his way.

* * *

Dr. Mason closed his bag with a snap. "Well, young lady, you have improved greatly since the first time I visited here." The doctor had arrived shortly after nuncheon to look at his patient.

Lady Cresswood stepped close to the bed as the doctor spoke. "That is excellent news, Doctor. How soon may we begin to allow Miss Hamilton to get up? I know she must be getting restless confined to bed."

"I see no reason for her to remain in bed if she has no headache." Dr. Mason turned to Miranda, shaking a finger at her as he ordered, "That does not mean you may resume all your normal activities like riding and the other things you young ladies enjoy so much. It means for you to try to walk a little and then rest with your foot up. Take it slowly and don't continue if you begin to feel dizzy. Your foot is healing nicely, but we must take care with your head injury."

Taking the glasses from his nose, Dr. Mason added, "If you should enjoy going downstairs, that will be quite all right as long as someone carries you down the stairway. You are not ready for that challenge as yet."

Lady Cresswood smiled delightedly at Miranda. "Is it not wonderful, Mary? You shall be able to join us for dinner soon. I feel sure the family will be pleased for you to enliven our drawing room. I fear Reggie is beginning to find us frightfully dull. He was actually talking about visiting Scotland soon. He, who vowed it is a land of underdressed upstarts!"

Miranda wasn't sure she wanted to be in company with the inhospitable Lord Cresswood. Then she was struck by her situation. "I should very much enjoy joining you for dinner, Lady Cresswood, but I fear my wardrobe is not sufficient to be at table with your family. I believe your nephew would say the same of me."

Pushing aside Miranda's objection, Lady Cresswood countered, "My dear, that shall present no problem. You may use some of Ellen's gowns, for you are much the same size. She has a closet full of dresses she rarely wears, so often is she in her riding habits. She can select several for you and I will let Sally make whatever alterations are needed today. You will look lovely, I promise you."

"Thank you," Miranda said quietly. She would have at least another day of peace before she must face the earl. Yet even though she wanted to avoid him, she longed to see his handsome face again.

"My dear, this is such a small thing for us to do for you. You have more than repaid us by encouraging Julian to forget joining the army. He told me of your talk this morning and I greatly appreciate all you said, for now he is talking of touring the West Indies with a tutor."

Miranda looked pleased. "I was certain that a mother would not wish the army for him."

Leaning forward Lady Cresswood kissed Miranda upon the cheek. "You have done the family a great service. We shall never forget."

The doctor cleared his throat to get her ladyship's attention, saying he must go and bidding his patient farewell. Lady Cresswood escorted him out, leaving Miranda to ponder how the earl felt about her interfering. She soon came to realize she mustn't borrow tomorrow's troubles today.

The rest of the day was spent enjoyably with visits from various members of the Benton family. She rose, resting on the sofa near the fire. Ellen had loaned Miranda a beautiful pink gown which very much suited her blond colouring.

Under the watchful eye of a maid and with Julian's help, she walked gingerly around the room until her ankle ached. The young man was quite enthusiastic. "One more time around the room. You can do it. Just be careful and take it slowly."

"I am being careful and taking it slowly. I begin to think 'tis you who are anxious for me to be out of the sickroom. Are you planning some grand adventure? Or have you gotten Lord Cresswood's permission to sail the seven seas?" she teased.

Julian helped her sit on the sofa, gently pushing an ottoman under her bound foot as she lifted it. His face took on a glum look. "I spoke with Mother this morning about the trip. Miller tells me my brother had a long conversation with her in the breakfast parlor, but he hasn't spoken to me. I think he probably presumes I am engaging in some maggoty whim. Not that I can blame him. I've made a cake of myself over the past year, getting into one scrape after another."

"Lord Cresswood must know all young men end up in the suds during their youth. My uncle told us many funny tales about his young officers. I should be much surprised if the earl had no missteps in his early days of cutting a dash in Society."

Julian laughed bitterly as he settled into a chair opposite. "No, I think he sprang upon Society a complete Corinthian."

Miranda suspected the younger Benton had spent his life in the shadows of a more accomplished older brother. No wonder he longed to make his mark in the world. "No doubt your mother could tell you some tales of the earl's passage into manhood which would make you realize mistakes are a part of learning. Don't be so hard on yourself. Give the earl some time to think about your plan. You have sprung it upon him rather suddenly. He will come to see that you are serious."

"Julian, serious?" the earl's voice came from the open door. "That will be a welcomed change."

"Charles!" Julian stood up, remembering to be on his best behavior for his brother, but his face flushed pink.

Miranda felt warm under the scrutiny of Lord Cresswood's cool grey eyes.

"Miss Hamilton, I understand from my mother you are to join us on the morrow."

"The doctor said I may, if I feel up to the trip downstairs."

"And if Julian doesn't loiter around all day chattering and tiring you out. Come, I believe dinner is soon to be served."

Julian flushed a deeper red. "I was just leaving, Charles. I shall see you later, Miss Hamilton."

As the young lord's footsteps rang in the hall, Lord Cresswood arched one dark brow, his gaze lingering on Miranda.

"Perhaps you should not encourage Julian to spend so much time in your room. It cannot do anything but impede your recovery. Good night, Miss Hamilton." The earl left Miranda's room without a backward glance.

So Lord Cresswood was still trying to keep her from his family. It was almost like a challenge in Miranda's mind. For the first time since the plan was mentioned, she was now looking forward to joining the family to perhaps rattle his lordship out of that cool reserve.

After dinner, she received a visit from Cousin Amelia. "You are starting to get the roses back in your cheeks, Mary. We shall have you well before you can count to three."

"Yes, I am starting to feel my strength return. Lady Cresswood insisted I come down to join the family tomorrow. That shall be delightful. I look forward to meeting Mr. Chartley."

"Yes, he is a charming young man, if something of a fribble. His attire is a delight to behold." The grey-haired lady didn't elaborate, leaving Miranda even more curious about the man with the scratched boots.

Ellen arrived in the late evening. She declared she had escaped the small talk of the drawing room in order to go to bed early so she might rise to ride. She was dressed in a lovely sea-foam green gown with dark green ribbons, which complimented her grey eyes—eyes which reminded Miranda of the earl.

"How do you like this shade of green, Mary? I think it's the right colour for me, but Mother insists that white is the only colour for a come out," Lady Ellen complained as she pivoted slowly for Miranda to see the lovely green gown with white pearls set on the bodice.

" 'Tis lovely, but your mother must know best. Are you to have a Season in the spring?" Miranda thought the girl looked too young.

"If I had my way, I would never go to London for a come out. I care nothing for dresses and dances and opera. Give me a good horse with clear skies and I am content."

Miranda was suddenly reminded of her beloved Baruq. She hoped the mare was recovering and being well fed. "I am a great lover of horses as well. But unfortunately, they fill only a small part of a lady's life."

"Too small a part, in my opinion. There is always sewing and pianoforte and visiting stuffy old neighbors. I should far better prefer the life of a gypsy, traveling the countryside in a colourful caravan with my animals. There is a band staying at the old mill even now."

Miranda was shocked. Clearly Lady Ellen had a great deal of growing up to do if she was enchanted by the hard life of gypsies. "My dear, I hope you do not romanticize the Romney. It would very soon get old to live in such close quarters. Too cold in winter, too warm in summer, moving always and ever reviled, whether rightly so or not. Promise me you will not go near any passing troupes."

"But they are said to have monkeys with them."

Still trying to discourage the naive child, Miranda said, "I do not know if there is any truth to the tales, but I hear the animals are trained to steal things."

The young lady looked disappointed, as if she'd not considered these aspects of gypsy life. "Perhaps you are right. But I still do not wish a Season."

Miranda was relieved to get back to the original subject. "Give yourself time. You are young yet. Things change as you get older." Not always for the better, as in Miranda's case, but things did change.

"Did you have a Season?" Ellen inquired as she sat upon the edge of the chair.

"No, I was in mourning for my mother when I turned eighteen. It was several years ago and I don't think of it now." Miranda heard the slightest note of regret in her voice.

"I am so sorry. It was a thoughtless question, for if you'd had a Season, you would likely be married instead of working as a governess, as lovely as you are. Please forgive me," Ellen begged with remorse.

Gently smiling at the young girl, Miranda vowed to get control of her melancholy. "There is nothing to forgive. When you are old enough, I should like you to go to Town and be the Belle of the Season so that I might tell my friends I am acquainted with a diamond of the first water."

Ellen laughed. "Don't be silly. I shall likely scandalize Society with some *faux pas* at my first ball."

"I predict when your time comes you shall take London by storm." Miranda thought Ellen excessively pretty as she blushed at the compliment.

Taking her leave, Ellen said good night. Miranda felt sure the young girl would change her mind about a Season when she was older.

That night as Miranda settled into bed, she was satisfied with the progress she'd made walking on her injured foot. It was an enjoyable day, and she felt she was getting stronger.

She very much liked Julian and Ellen Benton. As she thought of the family, her musings turned to Lord Cresswood. She knew he wouldn't be pleased that she had spoken with both his siblings today, but she'd enjoyed their visits. Then she wondered what it would be like to have the earl genuinely smile at her.

She spoke out loud in the darkness. "I must have been hit upon the head harder than I realized, to be thinking of a man who clearly dislikes me. Why do I keep thinking of him?" Turning over, she tried to push the proud earl from her mind as she drifted into sleep.

The following day was uneventful for Miranda. She had few visitors except for Amelia Warren and Lady Cresswood. She learned that the earl had taken his sister and brother off on some unscheduled trip. Being no fool, Miranda was certain it was to keep them out of her company.

By evening she was ready to attempt a foray downstairs. Sally pulled a lovely evening dress over Miranda's head as she steadied herself on the bedpost, standing quietly as the maid did up the buttons.

Miranda smoothed the beautiful white silk skirt down with her hands. "Sally, I cannot take this gown. It's far too beautiful for Lady Ellen to give up," she protested weakly.

"Never fear, Miss Hamilton. 'Twas Lady Ellen what selected the gown for you and you look lovely in it, if I may say so." Sally stood back to admire Miranda.

The dress fit her slender figure comfortably. "You have done a wonderful job of altering the gown. Thank you for your hard work."

Sally's face flushed pink with pleasure. "I very much enjoy needlework, Miss. I hope to get an opportunity to make clothes for a wee one when the earl marries."

Miranda's stomach tightened at the thought of his lordship's marriage. With a nonchalance she was far from feeling, she asked, "Is the earl betrothed?"

"No, Miss. I only meant when the time came. Now

sit down here and let me dress your hair. I'll keep it simple." Sally quickly began to brush Miranda's golden tresses, failing to note the relief on the girl's face. "That should do it," Sally said after a few minutes of work.

Miranda gazed at her reflection with a feeling of pride. The evening gown had a modestly cut square bodice of blue silk. A small white ruffle of lace stood up around the top of the bodice. The tiny puffed sleeves and the high-waisted skirt were white with three pale blue bands of ribbon at the hem. Sally had pulled her hair up to the top of her head, allowing ringlets to tumble down behind. She'd put a small spray of artificial blue flowers at the top of the knot.

Miranda knew she looked her best. She had not dressed so elegantly for dinner since her mother died. As she thought about how much she missed her dear mother, her throat tightened and tears came to her eyes. She chided herself about falling into self-pity as she wiped at the tears.

Thanking Sally again for all her work, Miranda accepted a blue cashmere shawl from the maid. A tap at the door startled Miranda and she turned.

The young maid ran to open the door. Standing in the doorway was Lord Cresswood. Miranda's knees felt weak and her hands trembled as she pulled the shawl around her shoulders. He stood gazing at her. For a moment, she thought she detected a hint of admiration in his face. If so, it was gone in a flash.

"Miss Hamilton," the earl said, his voice no more cordial than during their last encounter.

Lord Cresswood was the most handsome man she'd ever beheld. Elegantly dressed in black superfine and white waistcoat, the only ornamentation he wore was a single diamond in his white cravat. White pantaloons encased his manly legs. His black hair was brushed in a neat Brutus style. His slate grey eyes surveyed her questioningly.

Remembering her manners, she stuttered, "M-my lord . . . i-is there something you wished?" She was annoyed at her missish behavior.

"My mother requested I carry you down to the drawing room. Are you ready?" Cresswood asked in a neutral voice. His face gave no indication of his feelings.

Shocked, Miranda continued to stumble over her words. "But I thought . . . I mean, Lord Julian . . . or one of the footmen." Getting control of her tumultuous thoughts, she stood up straighter and calmly stated, "That would be asking too much, my lord. One of the male servants could easily carry me."

"Why, Miss Hamilton, do you doubt my ability to bring you safely to the drawing room?" Cresswood asked with a wolfish smile as he walked towards her.

Responding to the challenge in his manner, Miranda replied, "I do not doubt your ability to bring me safely to the drawing room, my lord. It is your desire for my safe arrival I question. I strongly suspect you would much prefer to drop me over the balustrade."

Smiling, he swooped her up into his arms. Their faces only inches apart, the earl spoke in a husky voice. "Fear not, Miss Hamilton, I have yet to murder a guest in my home . . . no matter how unusual the circumstances of their visit."

Time caught as a warm tingle rushed through Miranda. The earl peered into her eyes as if searching for some hidden secret. She was bewitched by him, and her mouth went dry and her palms grew wet. She sensed she evoked some strong effect on him when his arms tightened. As he continued to stand gazing into her eyes as if spellbound, the maid coughed.

The earl glanced at the girl by the door distractedly. Seeming to realize where he was, he walked out of the room, leaving Sally with a puzzled expression on her face.

Miranda felt breathless as the earl clutched her to him. Though her arms tightened comfortably around his neck as she held on, she was angry with herself for responding to his closeness. His very manner had made it clear he thought her some nefarious creature. She tore her gaze away from him and pretended to observe the portraits they passed in the long hall.

"Why so devoid of conversation, Miss Hamilton? I am surprised *you* are so quiet, with all the *good* advice you have seen fit to dispense to my brother and sister." The earl's voice was filled with sarcasm.

"As you can see, I cannot leave my room as yet under my own power. I did not seek out any member of your family, my lord. They have all come to me."

"So you felt it necessary to give them the benefit of your aged wisdom," the earl returned with clear disdain as he reached the head of the stairs and started down.

Staring at Lord Cresswood's handsome but rigid face, Miranda queried, "Is it that I gave them advice that angers you, my lord, or that they choose to listen to me where you have failed?"

"I should inform you that I have managed this family

rather nicely for almost thirteen years without your interference, Miss Hamilton," the gentleman returned coldly.

Something in the earl's voice made Miranda realize that she had touched a sensitive area. Her anger faded. When he reached the front hallway, she said, "Lord Cresswood, I do apologize if you think I overstepped my bounds, or gave your brother and sister bad counsel. 'Twas not my intention to interfere."

At the skeptical look on the earl's face, Miranda added, "Well . . . I *was* trying to help Lady Cresswood by discouraging the army in your brother's case, and surely you didn't wish your sister cavorting with gypsies. Are those such bad suggestions?"

They reached a set of double doors, which a liveried footman opened for them to enter. The earl carried Miranda into the elegantly appointed drawing room and placed her upon a blue satin sofa, his frown was now gone, replaced with a single raised eyebrow. "Indeed not. But why would my brother and sister heed a complete stranger when my mother and I have sought to convince them of the very thing, to no avail?" He stood back as his gaze searched her face.

Miranda arranged her skirts adroitly to cover her bound foot as she responded, "I can only tell you from my own experience. When I was fifteen, I purchased a bonnet I thought all the crack. My mother pleaded with me not to wear it, for it was above all things ugly and made me appear ridiculous. But I would not listen. When my governess returned from a visit with her mother, she immediately informed me that I would only wear it should I enjoy looking like a quiz. My mother had said all the same things, but in my youth, I thought I was grown up and my mother was merely trying to tell me what to do. It took someone who was not a family member to make me realize the truth. She said it was always the way with young people. The ones who loved them the most they heeded the least."

As she finished the story, the earl smiled, making her heart flutter at the sight. "What became of the offending hat?" he asked.

"I believe I burned it when my sanity returned," Miranda said with humor.

As the pair smiled at one another, the door to the drawing room opened and Julian entered. "Miss Hamilton, I am delighted to see you. I hope you will allow me to lead you in to supper this evening, since Charles got the opportunity to bring you down." He came to the sofa and took up a position at Miranda's right.

A frown appeared immediately upon the earl's countenance as he watched Miranda converse with his brother. Her heart sank, for whatever progress had been made with the earl's resolve to dislike her seemed to be lost.

Seven

Miranda wouldn't allow Lord Cresswood to ruin her first evening downstairs with his dark looks. Instead, she ignored him. She accepted the glass of claret a footman offered her and chatted with Julian as they awaited the others.

She soon had the opportunity to meet Mr. Reginald Chartley and heartily agreed with Mrs. Warren that he was a fribble, but a nice young man all the same. He took a position at her left. The earl, edged out by his cousin, moved to the mantel and took up a position to observe Miranda.

The lady gave all appearances of being genteel. He could not believe her to be Sir Peter's swindler. Still, this was his family he was protecting. He must be cautious.

"M-my dear M-Miss Hamilton, at last I get to m-meet the lady whom I've heard so m-much about."

Looking at Lord Cresswood, Miranda could only wonder at what the young man had been told about her. "Perhaps I should be safe and say 'tis likely that only half of what one normally hears is true."

Reggie puckered his thin brow as he considered the statement. "You know, I believe you are correct, for I'd swear that I saw Lord Anthony Dalton coming out Lady

Gregor's front door a sennight ago when he swore he'd been at White's all night."

Julian choked on his claret, and Cresswood, without so much as a bat of an eye at his naive cousin's inappropriate comment, changed the subject to the gentleman's new lavender carriage. Reginald was easily diverted to the subject and spent the remainder of the evening hanging on Miranda's sleeve, having found someone new to listen to all his old stories.

For Miranda's part, she was content to allow the young dandy to chatter away incessantly. It gave her an opportunity to observe the earl with his family. As the evening moved onward, the gentleman seemed to become more congenial and smiling. He laughed at the stories told by Julian and Reginald, spoke pleasantly with his mother and sister and kindly to Mrs. Warren.

Only once when the ladies retired to the drawing room, leaving the gentlemen to their port, did he shoot a questioning look at Miranda as if he meant to order the men to immediately follow, but something in the look which passed between him and Lady Cresswood caused him to relax back in his chair.

The gentlemen soon joined the ladies, but Miranda found herself fatigued. She'd barely completed her request to return to her room before the earl was there to scoop her into his arms, causing her heart to misbehave.

He carried her into the hall, then mounted the stairs. "So, Miss Hamilton, how did you enjoy your evening?"

Miranda looked suspiciously at the gentleman, but found no sarcasm or arrogance in his look or tone. Had he softened toward her? It appeared so. She desperately wanted it to be so.

"You have a delightful family, my lord. They do you proud."

For the first time ever, the earl smiled down at her. If it were possible, she would have been certain her heart had turned over in her chest. "I am very proud of my brother and sister. I think eventually they will find what they are looking for and settle down to happy lives."

Miranda gave a sigh. A happy life for her seemed quite far off at this exact moment. The thought of leaving the Bentons and Oakhill did not make her happy in the least.

Realizing the earl was regarding her closely, she struggled to say something. Uttering the first thing which came to her, she babbled, "Does Mr. Chartley visit often?"

Lord Cresswood's grey eyes darkened; then he looked straight ahead at the hallway. "I should perhaps warn you that Reginald's mother is expected any day. She is a woman who guards her son's life jealously."

Miranda was taken aback. Did the earl truly think she'd set her cap at the likes of Reginald Chartley?

Before she could make a reply to the startling insinuation, the gentleman stepped through the door to Miranda's bedroom and set her on her feet. With a formal bow, he bid her and her waiting maid good night and exited her room, leaving behind a baffled young lady.

Charles stood on the west terrace the following afternoon, watching the gardener prune the bushes in the miniature maze the fourth Earl of Cresswood had created as a gift for his bride. The unusually balmy November day had drawn him out into the fresh air, where he stood pondering his world.

Charles's mind was in a state of turmoil about Miss Hamilton. The beautiful young waif confused him with her pretty manners and appealing nature. She'd observed all the niceties throughout last evening. Somehow, the story she'd related about her governess had gone a long way to convincing him she was not Sir Peter's swindler. The tale had rung true. He liked the way she'd been able to laugh off her own foolish behavior regarding the bonnet.

The only dark spot upon the evening was Reginald. He'd dangled upon the girl's every word. Aunt Agatha would have Charles drawn and quartered if his cousin formed an alliance with a penniless girl, let alone one who might be far worse.

Cresswood knew there was more to the problem than his worries about Reggie. He was equally disturbed by the girl. As he'd entered her room last evening to carry her to the drawing room he'd been overwhelmed with the urge to kiss her delectable mouth. He actually forgot his suspicions about her as he held her to him. Worse, she'd even invaded his dreams last night. How could he expect Julian and Reginald to resist the chit when he was behaving like a greenhead himself?

"Where the devil are you, Peter? You could resolve all this uncertainty about the girl," the earl muttered to the gentle breeze. He'd received no reply to his letter and was baffled his messenger hadn't returned.

The sound of a door closing echoed through the garden. The earl turned to see his mother drift towards him with only a shawl covering her fashionable brown morning dress.

"Good day, dearest. I missed you at breakfast." The dowager countess came beside him and reached over to brush a dead leaf from the stone balustrade.

"I decided to get an early start. I went round to visit the vicar. But any schemes involving the curate must wait. It appears Mr. Halley is away at Sheffield at the moment. He will be gone for a week to stay with family because of the death of a relative. And before I forget, Reverend Wilton sent his regards."

"Did you fully explain to the vicar what you had in mind for Mr. Halley?"

"I felt it was only fair to inform the good vicar he would be without the curate for some time. In truth, I sensed a certain reluctance on his part, although he said nothing to dissuade me." The earl glanced pensively back at the landscape as he spoke.

A shadow of annoyance passed over the dowager countess's face. "You need not think the vicar shall support such a plan. Mr. Halley performs many of the parish duties. The reverend is a rather indolent man, for all that he has a good heart."

"Well, I didn't go to get his permission, but to ascertain if the curate was interested in such a position. The vicar would not be so unwise as to tell Halley he cannot go with Julian, for I should be very displeased," the earl finished sternly.

"You can be sure the vicar will support your decision once he discerns you intend enacting the plan. Did you speak with your brother about it?" Lady Cresswood looked up at him with a questioning gaze.

"I thought we should wait until we know if the curate is agreeable. I don't wish to get Julian's hopes up only for them to be dashed if Halley decides against such a journey. Who knows, sailing might make the young man ill, and not all young men crave adventure."

"True. I didn't consider that possibility. I think you are correct to delay telling Julian. 'Twould be too much of a disappointment should the plan not come to be. He was quite content last evening at home. 'Twas delightful to have Mary join us for dinner, was it not? She is a well-mannered young lady." She intently watched his response.

He nodded his head in agreement, but failed to tell her he thought Reggie was a trifle too charming for his own good. He needed to think of something to distract his cousin away from Miss Hamilton.

"I think it might be quite pleasant to have a dinner party. You might wish to invite Lord and Lady Frampton to dine with us tomorrow evening. I did not get a chance to see him on the last visit he made to Town. And he always gives me valuable advice about estate management."

With a careful nonchalance, he added, "Be sure to include their lovely daughters as well. I am sure Reggie would appreciate an opportunity to dazzle the ladies."

"An excellent idea! Julian can personally deliver a message when he returns from Crawley. But that shall leave the numbers at the table quite uneven," the dowager countess fretted as she grabbed at her bonnet to keep a gust of wind from taking it away.

Ignoring the problem of the seating, the earl asked with mild interest, "What business did Julian have in

Crawley?" He was pleased to find the boy not hovering at Miss Hamilton's side.

"I don't know. He borrowed some funds last evening, so he must be planning something. He left word with Miller he would return before dinner," the dowager countess replied, unconcerned.

"You should not continue to loan him money. I shall advance him some extra ready for this quarter when he returns. I think it important he learn to live within his means. I fear he spent much of his allowance on his fashionable attire."

The dowager countess chose not to pursue the subject. " 'Tis quite mild out today. I hope this pleasant weather lasts. 'Tis difficult to believe it snowed only a few nights ago."

Taking his mother's hand, he placed it upon his arm. "Shall we walk through the garden? We must take advantage of this glorious day, for there will be few such before spring." He led his mother away from the house, discussing changes she might wish to make in the garden.

Inside the house, the large clock in the hall struck the hour. Miranda surveyed the library as she waited for Mr. Chartley to make a move upon the chessboard. She'd been surprised after nuncheon alone in her room when Ellen had arrived with her cousin, who inquired if they might bring Miranda down to the library. No sooner were they settled in that large, well-appointed room than Miranda admired the chess set and Reginald challenged her to a game. He was always looking for a new opponent, since few had patience with him.

For Miranda's part, her previous meeting with the dandy made her decide the young man had little depth to his intelligence. Therefore, it astounded her to learn he possessed the skill to play chess. Reluctantly agreeing to play with the Tulip, she discovered him to be an able player, even if somewhat slow in his moves.

Ellen had tagged along to the library. She sat quietly by the fireplace, thumbing through a copy of *La Belle Assemblee*. She had pleaded no patience with the game when Reggie searched for a partner.

"I have m-my m-move," Reginald said as he edged his bishop forward.

Smiling, Miranda examined the board and immediately captured a pawn. "Your move again, Mr. Chartley."

The dandy tugged at his red waistcoat before he hunched forward, frowning as he studied the board. Chewing on his index finger, his eyes darted about the board, intent upon his next move.

As Miranda examined the intricately carved chessman she'd just taken, the outside door to the library opened, startling her. Lord Cresswood entered, pausing briefly to look at the pair at play. Miranda's heart lurched at him standing in the bright shaft of sunlight pouring through the portal where he'd halted. His windblown hair looked almost blue-black in the light as he removed his beaver hat and attempted to smooth the tendrils with his hand.

"Excuse me, I hope I do not disturb you." The earl sounded as formal as a barrister as he closed the door and moved towards his desk. Miranda could tell by his raised eyebrow he hadn't expect to find her with his cousin. "There is a rather pressing business matter I must attend to."

Reginald looked up. "Go right on with what you m-must do, for M-Miss Hamilton and I shall not heed any distractions."

"Is there a problem, Charles? You look so serious." Ellen peeked around the top of the high-backed chair by which she had been hidden.

With a smile for his sister, the earl's manner became less formal. "No, little one, I must simply find an old lease for one of the tenants. It was on the desk quite recently."

Miranda watched him as he shuffled the papers which sat to one side of the polished desktop. A tap sounded at the hall door, and a footman entered. Everyone looked up at the interruption. The earl asked, "Yes, Jim?"

"A message came for Mr. Chartley, my lord." The green-liveried footman handed the frowning dandy the note.

Reggie distractedly thanked the footman, who left with a bow, then broke the seal and began the arduous task of reading the message. Miranda noted his lips moved like a child's as he struggled to decipher the note.

Shyly she glanced back at the earl. That gentleman, now seated at his desk, was rifling through a drawer. A soft gasp drew her attention back to Reggie.

"Is the news bad, Mr. Chartley?" Miranda asked with concern as she observed his gloomy countenance.

"The worst p-possible. M-Mama arrives on the m-morrow. I would go to Uncle Sebastian's, but Aunt Lucilla warned me 'twill serve no p-purpose when I told her I m-might try to get further away from Town." He slumped dejectedly as the letter slipped through his fingers to the floor.

"I don't understand, sir. You want to avoid your mother?" Miranda asked. The earl had insinuated Reggie's mother was rather much the night before.

From the fireplace Ellen sourly said, "That is because you don't know Aunt Agatha."

"Egad, what m-must I do, Cresswood? She is sure to rake me over the coals for running out the way I did." Reggie stood up and began to wring his hands as he trod nervously before the desk.

Coming around to where his cousin paced, Cresswood placed a steadying hand upon the impassioned young man's shoulder. "Calm down, old boy. It shan't be as bad as you imagine. You must go ahead and get the meeting over with. Your nerves will only get worse the longer you postpone it."

Surprised, Miranda watched the pair. What had Reginald run out on? She glanced at Lady Ellen, who seemed to see nothing unusual in Reggie's anguished behavior, for she'd lost interest in her cousin's histrionics and again scanned her magazine.

Miranda wondered what sort of dragon Mrs. Chartley was for Reginald to be so upset by the mere mention of her pending arrival. Her attention slid back to the earl. As he tried to calm his cousin, his gaze strayed over the young man's shoulder and caught her bemused look. As she stared at his handsome face, an easy smile curled his lips.

With a look of wicked pleasure, Cresswood said, "But I forgot. The person who can solve your problem is here with us."

"What?" Reggie gasped with hope, scanning the room as if some larger-than-life human had arrived.

"Miss Hamilton provides solutions to the most personal dilemmas. She is quite good at dispensing advice."

Miranda blushed at the pointed reference to her suggestions to Julian and Ellen, but she was not a young lady to back down from a challenge. Tilting her head back defiantly, she said, "I should very much like to assist you, Mr. Chartley. But I fear I know nothing of your mother; therefore I could offer you no useful advice, sir."

Lord Cresswood pursued the issue with apparent relish. "Reggie, you must describe the lady to Miss Hamilton so she might give you the answer to your problems."

"Describe? What do you m-mean, Cresswood?" Reggie looked to the earl with baffled eyes.

"Tell her about your mother's nature, how she acts around you," the earl said, never taking his gaze from Miranda's face.

The dandy's own face twisted strangely at the difficult mental task of describing his mother for them. "Well . . . she is spirited . . . and hard to control . . . wants m-me to always follow her lead . . . er . . . and frightening. Definitely not broken to the bit." Miranda heard Ellen giggle as they all listened to the incoherent speech.

"Good heavens, Mr. Chartley, it sounds more like you are describing a horse than your mother." Miranda's eyes sparkled with amusement as she gazed at the flustered young man.

"That should not discourage you from giving Reggie the answer to the problem of a tyrannical parent."

With exasperation at the earl's teasing, Miranda was

about to decline any comment when an idea occurred to her. "Do you ride, Mr. Chartley?"

"Ride? Yes, P-Papa p-put me on a horse when I was just a lad. Don't do m-much m-more than a turn round the p-park these days. The open air wilts m-my cravats." Reggie's hand came up to check the folded linen.

Miranda noticed his stutter became more pronounced as his agitation grew. "Do you remember the most important thing your father told you about your horse?" She avoided looking at the earl. She didn't want to know what he was thinking about her infernal meddling.

Furrowing his brow with deep concentration, Reggie suddenly smiled. "Yes, I remember. He said not to let Dusty graze on the front lawn. M-my pony tore holes in the grass, m-made M-mama furious."

Miranda dropped her gaze to the chessboard for fear if she looked at Cresswood she would laugh. She said, "Yes, I am sure that was an important issue, especially with your mother. But I was thinking about the point which all horsemen must know to ride successfully. The rider should always be the one in control. If you allow a horse his head, he will lead you down the path of his choosing, but when you keep a tight rein, the horse will obey."

Perplexed, Reggie said, "Are you saying I should treat my m-mother like a stubborn horse?"

With a gentle smile, Miranda said, "Not exactly, for your mother might take exception to the use of a riding crop, but if you make a decision and let your mother know there can be no argument, she shall come to accept that decision. You are a grown man and can no longer be ordered about as a child."

As Reggie rubbed his forehead in reflection, leaving his blond curls disordered, she briefly glanced at the earl. His face held a look somewhere between disbelief and admiration.

"I am not certain it shall work with M-Mama," Reggie offered after a few moments.

Lord Cresswood stepped forward and clapped a hand on his cousin's shoulder. " 'Tis what I recommend each time you lament your plight, Reggie, although not with such an interesting illustration. You must make it known to Aunt Agatha you shall no longer be bullied into her bidding. It shan't happen overnight, but inevitably she must come to realize you are a grown man on the Town."

"I shall try. But I m-must go and speak with Aunt Lucilla, for her advice is always sound." The young man left Miranda and the earl staring at one another with amusement after his abrupt departure.

"Well, that was quite rude of Reggie to leave you when your game was not complete." Ellen put the magazine on the nearby table and rose, frowning after her departing cousin.

" 'Tis of no consequence. I think he is quite distracted at present and would make a poor playing companion," Miranda excused the young man.

"Miss Hamilton, how does one get to be so wise at such a tender age?" The earl leaned upon his desk, arms folded across his broad chest, his voice amused.

Wise? Not the word Miranda would use to describe herself when she thought of her situation, masquerading as someone else with her stepbrother searching for her. She simply answered, "I believe losing my parents at an early age caused me to gain some maturity beyond my years, my lord. But you must understand Mr. Chartley will certainly not change overnight, if at all. It is difficult to deal with an intractable parent. They are more intimidating than any other person we deal with in life." She thought of her stepfather as she spoke.

"I cannot say, for Ellen and I were blessed with excellent parents," Cresswood said as he eyed her with a thoughtful look. "You speak as though you experienced such as Reggie."

"Not a parent, but a stepparent. 'Tis a painful subject." She could feel the earl's eyes upon her averted face as she pretended to examine the state of the chess game.

Coming to stand by the chess table, Ellen said, "Seems to me we are keeping you from your important business, Charles. Mama informed me earlier we host the Framptons tomorrow. I think Mary and I will go plan what we shall do for entertainment. Shall each of the ladies play a selection upon the piano, or would you care to sing?"

"You are having company?" Miranda was disconcerted at the news. The fewer people who knew she was at Oakhill, the better for her.

"Did Mother not tell you? Yes, one of our neighbors, but I cannot say we are often in their company, for the ladies spend much of their time in Town. It shall be a tolerable evening, but there will be no dashing gentlemen to amuse us, for there are no sons," Ellen lamented to Miranda.

"I shall remember that unkind remark when next you

are angling for a new horse." Cresswood spoke with a twinkle in his eyes.

"Oh, Charles, you know I did not mean that you are not top of the trees, but you are my brother and therefore you don't count."

"First I am not dashing and now I learn that I don't count. You wound me severely, little one." The earl grinned and clutched his chest as if in pain.

"I do no such thing. You are only wanting me to sing your praises before Mary, but she will have an aversion to us if we sit around vainly complimenting one another. Now, Mary, as I was saying, shall it be the piano or singing for you?" Ellen ignored her brother's teasing.

"I prefer it to be the piano. My singing is only passable." Miranda suffered with mixed emotions about the coming party. She was glad to be out from under the earl's scrutiny as he looked at his sister.

"Then we must go to the main drawing room and find a selection to perform from the music there. I will help you," Ellen said as she stepped forward and offered Miranda her arm.

As the injured girl rose, the earl queried doubtfully, "You play the piano, Miss Hamilton?"

With pride she said, "Yes, my lord. I have enjoyed playing since I was a small child." It was one of the few feminine skills in which Miranda knew she excelled.

"Then I look forward to your performance." Cresswood bowed.

As the two girls slowly left the room, Miranda glanced back to see the earl gazing at her at her thoughtfully.

* * *

Some hours later, Miranda sat with a book open on her lap. She'd spent the last half hour quietly trying to read it—she had carried it with her for several days—but visions of the earl's handsome face kept coming between her and the words on the pages as she daydreamed. The sound of a squeaking door drew her attention. Julian Benton's head slowly came into view as if he wanted to see into the room, but not be seen by the occupant.

"There you are, Miss Hamilton. I hoped to find you alone." The young man straightened and entered the Green Drawing Room, carrying a round box jauntily at his side.

"Please call me . . . Mary. I think we can dispense with the formalities, don't you?"

"Yes, I should like that very much, if you will call me Julian. Now, how is it that I am lucky enough to find you by yourself?" Julian came to the sofa where Miranda sat with her injured foot propped up. He placed the box on the table beside her and took a seat in the opposite high-backed chair which she indicated.

"Your mother and sister are quite busy preparing for the Framptons' visit on the morrow. Are they old friends of the family?" Miranda smiled inquiringly at Julian.

"My parents and the Framptons knew each other quite well at one time, but I have not met the daughters above a dozen times. I was surprised when I returned from Crawley and Mother asked me to take an invitation to them at once, but I would guess she wants to make it a little more entertaining for both you and Reggie."

Miranda frowned at Julian. "I hope she didn't go to trouble for me. I am quite content to remain quietly here recovering." She didn't want news of her presence to be in the neighborhood for fear Sylvester would hear of the mysterious female visitor at Oakhill, should he still be about.

"I understand it was Charles's suggestion. He and Lord Frampton often have dinner in Town to discuss agricultural management. His lordship is quite noted for running a bang-up estate."

Relieved the dowager countess was not going to so much trouble merely for her, Miranda said, "I am glad, for I should hate to inconvenience your mother."

Julian stood up and went to the box. "Mother enjoys entertaining, so think nothing of the party. Now, I had another reason for wanting to see you. I have something for you." He opened the box and pulled out a new black high-crowned bonnet.

"Julian, you should not have spent your money on a new bonnet for me. Sally is very clever with a needle. She could help me put new ribbons on my old one." Miranda took the bonnet as she spoke, admiring the lovely lace inset in the bill.

"No. After all you have been through, I thought it only fair that I replace the damaged one. You have not seen your old bonnet. I assure you it needed more than ribbons to make it presentable again. Ellen told me of a milliner in Crawley, so I rode over this afternoon and selected one. Do you like it?" Julian waited with a look of anticipation for her answer.

"It is very pretty and much nicer than the one I damaged. I am not sure I should be accepting gifts from you, however, even though it is most kind of you and I like it very much."

A slight flush came to Julian's face, and he let his

gaze fall to the floor. "In truth, it is from my mother, for my pockets are to let until next quarter. You would not refuse such a gift from her, would you?"

In the face of the young man's persistence, Miranda replied, "No, I would not be so ungracious."

She liked his beaming countenance much better as he looked back at her and smiled at her acceptance of the bonnet. Miranda handed the hat to Julian, who put it back in the box.

"I am pleased I was able to do some small thing to make up for the accident. This bonnet is just a meager way for me to say I am sorry." Julian looked guilty.

Taking his hand from the box in both of hers, Miranda said, "Whenever I wear it I shall fondly remember the Benton family and their great kindness to me. You are like a wonderful brother, Julian."

As the pair smiled at one another in harmony, a sardonic voice interrupted, "Do I intrude?" Cresswood stood at the doorway frowning. Beside him stood a tall elderly woman with an exceedingly long face. She was dressed all in black and peered at the pair with a look of censure.

Miranda released Julian's hand as if she had been burned. She had no reason to feel guilty, for Julian had left the door open, but the look on the earl's face made her heart ache. It was clear he thought the worst.

Julian turned to his brother with a relaxed smile. "No, for I was just giving Mary a replacement for her ruined bonnet. I destroyed her other one in the accident. Hello, Aunt Agatha. We were expecting you to arrive on the morrow."

Miranda noticed the frown deepen on Cresswood's

face as his brother called her Mary. Reginald's mother
eyed her with a look of caution.

"I am sure Reggie simply read the letter wrong. I
have come to believe he takes delight in vexing me.
Where is my wayward son?" she asked sternly. By the
martial light in the matron's eyes, Miranda could see the
dandy was in for a rare trimming.

"I believe he took out one of Charles's horses. Said
something about needing to practice his riding control.
I am uncertain what he was talking about, but I am sure
he shall return quite soon. The outdoors don't suit him."
Julian's face lost its smile as he spoke to his aunt.

Miranda smiled at the earl when Julian mentioned
Reggie's riding, but received only a cold look in return.
She appeared to be in his black books once again.

Cresswood led his aunt farther into the room saying,
"Please allow me to introduce my aunt, Miss Hamilton.
This is Mrs. Agatha Chartley, Reggie's mother, of whom
you have heard us speak. Aunt Agatha, this is Miss
Hamilton. She is staying with us while she recovers from
an accident."

Agatha Chartley raised her lorgnette to gaze at Miranda. "Hamilton? Any kin of Sir Howard Hamilton of
Brighton?"

"No, Mrs. Chartley. I do not know the gentleman."

Miranda saw she was deemed of no importance when
the lady dropped her glasses and turned to Cresswood.
"I simply must rest before dinner. This rushed trip has
quite shattered me. Send Reggie to me when he returns."
The lady turned and left the room, calling for Miller as
she went.

Cresswood made no comment about his aunt's abrupt

behavior. Instead he sternly gazed at his brother, who was putting the lid back on the hatbox. "Julian, in the future you might want to remember it does Miss Hamilton's reputation no good for you to be closeted with her alone in the drawing room."

"But I left the door open," Julian explained as he glanced back at her with a look of appeal.

Miranda was suddenly irritated with the earl. Each time she thought he was beginning to trust her, or at least not dislike her, some new incident made him glower at her again. She decided not to be embarrassed by the situation he and Mrs. Chartley found them in. Coming to Julian's defense, she stated, "I was merely thanking your brother for being so thoughtful. He rode all the way to Crawley this morning to get me a new bonnet. It was most kind." She smiled at Julian again.

"Yes, Julian, it was kind of you, but please make sure that Ellen or Mother is with Miss Hamilton before you intrude upon her again."

Miranda was surprised when Julian meekly replied, "Yes, Charles."

The earl spoke more kindly to his brother. "You might want to go find Reggie. You know what Aunt Agatha can be like if he keeps her waiting above twenty minutes."

A look of understanding came into Julian's face as he begged to be excused. He left the earl and Miranda alone.

Miranda shifted uncomfortably on the sofa as the earl gazed at her. Expecting a reprimand, she was not disappointed.

"Miss Hamilton, I know little of your upbringing, but I can tell you it is not proper to closet yourself with my brother—or any other gentleman, for that matter. However—"

Anger surged through Miranda. She'd had enough of this arrogant lord sneering down his nose at her. He might not know it, but he was addressing an earl's daughter. Rising with as much dignity as she could muster, she interrupted the earl's speech. "Sir, I have little control over your brother. I was here quietly reading when he joined me. There can be no objection to our conversing with a footman in the hall observing us. Mayhap if you were to give me the benefit of the doubt where it comes to my behavior, we might deal with each other more civilly."

Limping forward, she yanked the hatbox from the table. The sudden movement caused the table to rock precariously. A lovely statuette of the goddess Athena, which sat to the side of the table, began to topple to the floor.

Dropping the box, Miranda rushed to catch the falling figurine. Her hands clutched it desperately, but the weight took her by surprise. She feared she would not be able to hold on, but then the earl's hands closed over hers.

Her hands were crushed beneath his stronger ones. Miranda gazed up into the earl's handsome face as her heart pounded at his touch. His eyes intently scrutinized her, as if he could read some hidden message in her heart.

As a deep blush stained her face, she uttered, "I am so sorry, my lord. I fear I allowed my temper to get the better of me. I should very much regret breaking any of Lady Cresswood's lovely pieces."

"I know it was an accident, Miss Hamilton." The earl's voice sounded husky as he stood before her with the marble goddess between them, their hands touching.

He placed the sculpture upon the table, and Miranda felt a sense of loss when the earl's hands left hers. She dropped her arms to her side and stepped back as his nearness made the blood pound in her ears.

They gazed at one another in silence for a few moments before the earl broke the spell. "Until this evening, Miss Hamilton."

Miranda watched his retreating figure, wondering about the intriguing man. Occasionally he seemed to forget his dislike of her, as in the library earlier, but too often he seemed to think her some low person come to taint his family. She really couldn't blame him. He still knew nothing of her, but, oh, how she longed for those times when he smiled at her. With a sigh, she picked up the hat box and limped from the room.

Eight

Surveying the gathered company with a jaundiced eye, Cresswood stood at the elegant mantel the following evening. The Benton family and their guests were scattered about the Rose Drawing Room in small groups. He'd encouraged his mother to invite Lord Frampton and his family because of their two eligible daughters, hoping to distract both Julian and Reggie away from Miss Hamilton by adding an array of lovely young ladies. His plan had gone awry.

Lady Maude and Lady Esther, Lord Frampton's daughters, were both passably pretty, endowed with dusky curls and dark brown eyes, clad in the first style of elegance. Like many fashionable chits, they were interested in titles and money. As a second son, Julian held no allure, and Reginald was a plain mister with only a modest fortune.

After the arriving guests were introduced to the assembled group and given refreshments, they broke into small clusters around the drawing room. Somehow Frampton's daughters attached themselves to a group which surrounded him, leaving Julian and Reggie to pursue their own interests.

Cresswood picked up his glass of claret from the

nearby table as he continued to appraise the assembled company. To his left, Lady Cresswood sat with the elderly marquis and his lady wife, clearly enjoying the reunion with her old friends. They comfortably reminisced about old times when Cresswood's father was alive. The earl knew his mother didn't share his fears about the dangers of Miss Hamilton's beauty attracting Julian. She paid scant attention to her youngest son.

Beyond his mother's group sat Reginald with his mother. He'd survived the stormy meeting with his irate parent, but showed no resolve to stand up to the lady.

Aunt Agatha lingered protectively by her son's side, whispering in his ear, determined to keep any female she didn't approve of away from him. She had questioned Cresswood at length about the two female guests' expectations upon marrying, when told of the dinner party. The earl thought it ironic she completely dismissed the threat of the most beautiful lady in the room as insignificant.

As he took a sip from his glass, Cresswood's gaze paused on the lovely countenance of his sister. A gentle smile came to his lips as he noted the white muslin dress she'd donned for the party. She had vowed it was not her colour.

Ellen sat beside Lady Maude and across from Lady Esther on one of the sofas directly in front of the fireplace. His sister valiantly attempted to hold the fashionable ladies' interest. They, however, were intently trying to flirt with him, casting languishing looks in his direction.

He looked up to see Julian and Miss Hamilton. The earl's grip tightened on the glass with frustration. The pale blue evening gown she wore enhanced her captivating eyes as she briefly glanced at him. She looked very desirable.

Somehow, the pair had managed to drift over to a sofa near the piano and were involved in a private conversation. Cresswood could see they were content with the situation as Julian laughed at a lively comment made by his pretty companion.

Watching his brother's animated face, Cresswood considered whether he should tell the boy the proposed trip had his endorsement. The anticipated event might prevent him from doing anything foolish, like losing his heart where Miss Hamilton was concerned.

The earl was contemplating joining the *tete-a-tete* when Lady Maude drew him back into her conversation. " 'Tis true, is it not, my lord?"

"Pardon me, I was distracted for a moment. What were you saying?" Reluctantly the earl brought his gaze back to the young woman he would describe as attractive rather than pretty.

"I told Lady Ellen that Esther and I never saw you at the fashionable balls and routs. You were quite elusive during the past Season. I think I caught a glimpse of you at the Fordyces' soiree, but only for a moment. 'Twas such a squeeze I nearly fainted, and poor Esther's gown was badly crushed. I believe you accompanied Sir Peter Weldon on that occasion." Lady Maude peered up at him from beneath her lashes.

"I fear the balls and routs grow rather tiresome after so many Seasons. You will find it so when you have experienced even half the number I have." The earl glanced up when he heard another round of laughter from the direction of his brother. He longed to sit where

Julian was, instead of making polite conversation with insipid chits. His brother didn't appear bored in the least.

"But, Charles, you tell *me* I must have a Season," Ellen pouted prettily.

"So you must, little one. When the time comes, you will be quite eager. I look forward to seeing the Season through your unjaded eyes." He cast his sister a reassuring smile. Taking a sip of his claret, he used the opportunity to glance over the glass's rim to his brother and Miss Hamilton.

Lady Esther took her turn at trying to bewitch the earl. Fluttering her eyes, she said, "Then you must be sure to come to our first ball of the Season, my lord, and bring your friend Sir Peter, as well as your lovely sister. I daresay his mother shall be quite recovered from her frightening adventure by spring."

Cresswood was filled with uneasiness as his full attention settled upon the flirtatious miss. "Has some disaster befallen Lady Weldon?"

Lady Esther's eyes grew bright at the question and she appeared pleased to impart the gossip. She leaned forward eagerly. "My lord, it was the talk of the *ton* this past week. Even with Town so thin of company, it created quite a stir. Sir Peter rushed home to Carlisle, for his mother and sister were waylaid by highwaymen. The brigands stole the Weldon emeralds. Lady Weldon took to her bed and is reported gravely ill. I am surprised Sir Peter did not inform you."

"I would assume his plate is full taking care of his family. I was awaiting a letter from him any day about another matter. It is not surprising I received no communication. But I read nothing of this in the *Morning Post.*"

"I believe Sir Peter tried to keep it quiet, but you know how servants will gossip." Lady Maude spoke with a superior tone as she smoothed a wrinkle in her dress.

The earl glanced at Miss Hamilton who had tilted her head closer to Julian to speak. His eyes tracked a golden curl brushing against her ivory cheek, darkening when he thought of tracing his lips along the same path. Startled at where his thoughts were leading, he took a drink of claret and forced his attention back to the conversation.

Sir Peter was now in the north with his family. As the full impact of this penetrated his befuddled thoughts, Cresswood knew this was the worst possible news he could receive. Hadn't he put all his doubts in that section to rest? Not entirely. But he could not ask his friend to abandon Lady Weldon at such a time. If the ladies hadn't been present, he would have sworn soundly.

"Were the Runners called in?" The earl made an effort to continue to determine the seriousness of Peter's situation and push the beguiling Miss Hamilton from his mind.

Artfully opening her fan, Lady Maude continued the gossip. "Yes, Papa actually saw two Red Breasts following Weldon's coach out of London. 'Tis all so unbelievable. Do you think they will get the jewels back?"

"It is difficult to say, since I know so little of the episode. You say neither of the ladies was harmed?"

"Papa said he heard the lady became ill afterwards," Lady Esther piped. The sisters seemed to be taking turns telling the tale.

"Yes, I think it would shatter any delicately bred female." Cresswood knew Peter's mother to be a fragile widow who, the earl suspected, used her illnesses to manipulate her only son, but she might truly be laid low by such a robbery. He would dispatch a letter in the morning to Peter's estate explaining the situation at Oakhill and inquiring after the dowager's health. He desperately needed his questions about Mary Hamilton answered.

"Yes, I would never be so foolish as to travel without a gentleman for escort." Lady Maude fluttered her eyes invitingly.

"I am sure your father would not allow anything to happen to you, ladies." Cresswood looked musingly down at the glass of liquid he held, his distracted thoughts on his friend.

Miss Hamilton's gentle laughter drew the earl's notice. Julian gestured with his hands during a story as the lady gazed at the boy as though enthralled. Cresswood decided he would wait no longer.

As Ellen leaned forward and asked Lady Maude at what modiste she and her sister shopped for their lovely gowns, Cresswood excused himself.

Placing the nearly empty glass upon the mantel, he moved toward his brother and Miss Hamilton. He was surprised to receive a welcoming smile from each and felt a foolish sense of pleasure to know the lady was pleased for him to be there. "Julian, shall we trade partners? You might want to do the pretty with the other guests and entertain Lady Maude and Lady Esther."

For the second time in as many days, Julian did the earl's bidding with no complaint. Cresswood watched his brother join the group at the fireplace. He suspected the boy was on his best behavior while waiting to hear if his proposed plan was acceptable. Perhaps it was best to delay telling Julian a while longer to keep his brother so malleable.

Turning to Miss Hamilton, the earl asked, "May I?" gesturing at the vacant seat beside her.

"Please, I should enjoy the company." The girl's eyes scanned his face intently as she gazed up at him.

"How are you feeling, Miss Hamilton?" he asked with genuine interest.

She dropped her gaze to her bound foot propped upon a velvet footstool. "I am improving daily, my lord. I should be ready to leave soon." The earl thought he detected a note of wistfulness as she spoke.

"And are you feeling well enough to endure an evening's entertainment? I know Ellen plans for you to play the piano later." He watched her slender fingers tangle in the tassels on her borrowed fan.

Miss Hamilton tilted her head to look at him with a teasing smile. "If you don't wish me to play, my lord, I can come down with a severe case of colic after dinner. I should like to try my hand at amateur theatrics. Or shall it be a gentle swoon as the ladies leave the dining room?"

"No, indeed, Miss Hamilton. I look forward to your performance. You shall have to save your acting for some other occasion. Besides, I would not have my guests think Cook poisoned you. It puts rather a damper on one's party, don't you think?" The earl answered her teasing tone in kind, losing himself in her exquisite blue eyes.

"Quite true. I would not want to be responsible for that. Then I shall do my best to play as competently as the other ladies."

Cresswood liked the way her eyes twinkled up at him. "You may wish you truly were beset with the colic after sitting through Ellen's playing. I fear she has much more enthusiasm for horses than for the pianoforte." The earl cast his sister an indulgent glance before looking back at his partner.

"I come to think you are a hard critic, sir. It makes me quake to think what you shall say of my playing if you would say such of your beloved sister."

The door to the room opened and a dignified Miller intoned, "Dinner, my lord."

Cresswood looked at his companion. "I come to believe there is very little that would frighten you, Miss Hamilton." He noticed her lovely eyebrows rise as he excused himself to escort Lady Frampton and his mother.

The company assembled to move into the dining room. The shortage of gentlemen required they each escort two ladies. He looked past Lady Frampton to see that Julian escorted Ellen as well as Miss Hamilton. With a sense of relief, he knew he would not have to worry about his brother or his cousin during dinner, since his mother informed him earlier she had placed the young lady next to Frampton.

As he led his mother and Lady Frampton through the hallway, he asked himself if he was worried about his brother's welfare or merely envious of the time the boy spent with their beautiful houseguest. Perhaps it was best not to question himself too closely.

Miranda sat at nearly the opposite end of the table from Cresswood, but was very aware of his presence.

She was between Lord Frampton and Cousin Amelia.
She found the old marquis to be a charming gentleman,
but speaking with Mrs. Warren gave her an opportunity
to observe Lord Cresswood.

The dark blue superfine coat the earl wore made his
eyes look smoke grey in the glittering candlelight. She
liked watching the way his sculpted mouth curved into
a smile when something amused him. In the drawing
room earlier when he actually had given her a compliment—leastwise it seemed a compliment to Miranda—
she'd been pleasantly surprised.

Cousin Amelia claimed her attention. "Mary, you
seem to be improving rapidly. I believe if the mild
weather holds, you might enjoy sitting out on the terrace
tomorrow." The thin lady relished a bite of her sliced
roast beef.

"I should like that very much. I enjoy being out of
doors and spent much time in the fresh air back home."

"Well, I know Julian wants to take you driving, but
the earl has been sending him on numerous errands of
late. If the young scamp is too busy, we might get Mr.
Chartley to take you for a short jaunt if the airing tomorrow does you no harm. I understand he brought his
new coach from Town. He longs to have someone admire it, but I am afraid we all are continually occupied
with other things."

Miranda looked up to see the earl observing her conversation. A tentative curve of her lips was rewarded
with an answering smile before Lady Frampton claimed
his attention.

Bringing her regard back to Mrs. Warren, she said, "I
should very much like to see Mr. Chartley's coach. There

is such a stylish flare about him that I believe his coach must be quite unique."

"I cannot say, but I would expect anything he owned to be of the first stare. I know he would enjoy taking you for a drive. A short spin might be just the thing for you. We would not want to send you to London and have you develop a terrible headache from all the rattling about one gets while traveling. This can be a gentle testing of your stamina. I shall speak to Mr. Chartley in the morning."

As Mrs. Warren became engrossed in her meal, Miranda turned to her other partner. "My lord, you have two delightful daughters. You must be quite proud to have them on your arm during the Season." Miranda thought to make pleasant conversation. In truth, she disliked the way Lady Maude and Lady Esther simpered at the earl. It irritated her greatly, although she was not sure why.

The old marquis looked across at his girls with pride. "Yes, they are lovely, but I ain't much of one for all that Town foolishness. I leave it in Lady Frampton's capable hands. Would rather spend the better part of the Season here at my place, Windcrest."

"I hear you run an excellent estate, my lord. Lord Julian told me you are considered one of the best landholders in England. He said the earl very much respects your opinion on estate management."

"That so?" The old man beamed. "Well, I try to watch my fellows closely. Must say Cresswood runs a very tidy estate as well. You can never be too careful about watching over bailiffs. Mine is quite reliable, but I like to ride round the estate and keep an eye on things.

You never know what odd happening you might find."
The old man stared into space as he unconsciously
rubbed his chin in a pensive gesture. He distractedly
speared a small potato with his fork as if some problem
perplexed him.

Miranda gave the marquis a questioning glance. "You
sound as if some unusual occurrence troubles you, my
lord."

"Yes, that it does. Found some coxcomb in one of my
empty tenant houses the other day. Left the building vacant after old Brown died. Came to see what repairs
were needed before the new tenant arrived. Fellow
claims he is Redford's son."

In the act of sipping wine, Miranda choked slightly
as her stepbrother's name was mentioned. She brought
her napkin up to pat her lips and to stifle the frightened
cry which came to her throat. The marquis paused to
see if she was all right. Assuring him she was fine, she
took a minute to catch her breath. She struggled to keep
her voice calm as she spoke. "You were saying someone
was on your property. Did he say what he was after?"

"Humph, the cawker said he was looking for lands to
purchase. But I was at Eton with his father and he was
never so plump in the pockets that I remember. Besides,
I heard the old man owned an estate down near the coast
somewhere. Always was tight with his blunt and I never
thought he was an ivory turner, so his estate must still
be solvent. Heard the old fellow married several times,
but I don't think either was an heiress."

Lord Frampton touched his napkin to his mouth. "It
makes no never mind, for none of my lands are for sale.
I put a flea in his ear and sent him on his way. Expect

he shall know better than to lurk around Frampton lands again. It was all very havy-cavy."

Miranda's appetite fled. Sylvester was in the neighborhood. She was determined to find out all she could. "What was it you think the gentlemen was truly after?" she asked, fear knotting inside her.

Frampton sat back, resting his hands on the table. "I was puzzled at first. I knew there was nothing of value in the cottage or the old barn where I found him. Later, I stopped at the Pelican, an inn in East Grinstead with excellent homebrew." The old marquis's eyes glistened as he mentioned the ale. "The innkeeper said the boy had skulked round the neighborhood for a few days, first at the Grey Swan, then at the Pelican. He keeps spreading this humbug tale about buying property, but no one's been approached with an offer that I have heard, and there are several nice estates for sale. My coachman talked with his cousin at the Grey Swan and he claims the fellow first seemed to be looking for some relative and only later mentioned property, but it is all too smoky for me." Frampton seemed to dismiss the man from his thoughts, and his face cleared as he picked up his wine glass.

"Cresswood maintains excellent cellars. Need to find where he got his wine stock." The old man took a deep drink, then gestured the footman to refill his glass.

"Is the gentleman still in the neighborhood?" Miranda distractedly stirred the food upon her plate with her fork.

"No, one of the grooms came back from East Grinstead this morning and the innkeeper said Redford had left for London. Good riddance. I made it my business to watch the sneaky fellow, because I always thought his father a trifle shady, as well."

Miranda felt the knot in her stomach ease. Her stepbrother had been in the area searching for her. She actually owed Julian a debt of gratitude for running her down. He'd inadvertently placed her where her stepbrother would never think to look.

Glancing back at the handsome earl at the end of the table, Miranda hoped he would not get wind of her stepbrother's activities. At least Sylvester was in London for the present.

As the earl looked up and their gazes caught, she realized her time at Oakhill was getting short. His eyes seemed to darken as they moved over her face, and Miranda sensed some message lying in their somber grey depths. The moment passed as the earl turned to speak with his aunt.

As she concentrated on her plate, Miranda's shoulders slumped. She must leave with this masquerade between them. She wished she could tell the earl and his family her true identity. But Lord Redford would have her in his power until she married or turned five and twenty, and he seemed more determined than ever to find her. She glumly stared at her plate and knew her evening had been ruined.

Agatha Chartley sat with the younger ladies in the drawing room as the women waited for the gentlemen to join them. Miranda realized someone had told Reginald's mother she was a governess, for the lady had treated her with a certain condescension since their meeting yesterday. She even made an effort to exclude Miranda from the group of young ladies as they came into the drawing room.

Miranda was more amused than offended. She was coming to understand what it was going to be like for the next few years until she came into her fortune and could move about Society as the daughter of an earl. Penniless young ladies were not welcomed into the *ton*.

Sitting with Lady Cresswood and Lady Frampton, Miranda listened to them discuss the happenings in Crawley and the neighborhood. Being unfamiliar with the area, she contributed little to the discussion. She needed time to herself to get her nerves under control after the revelations of Lord Frampton. Sylvester would not give up the search easily, but she had not thought he would linger so long in the immediate area.

"Mary?" The dowager countess smiled at Miranda.

"I apologize, Lady Cresswood. I fear I was woolgathering. Did you have a question?" Miranda's cheeks warmed with embarrassment.

"We wondered if you had selected a piece for the piano tonight." The dowager countess reached over and patted Miranda's folded hands maternally.

"Lady Ellen and I each chose a piece of music yesterday and practiced. I hope we shall not drive anyone from the room with any misplayed notes." Miranda opened her fan to cool her warm cheeks.

Leaning close so the other ladies would not hear, Lady Cresswood confided, "I fear we must be prepared for a few from Ellen. She loves the piano, but detests the practicing. I have told her she must spend more time at the keys if she wants to perform acceptably in company.

Unfortunately, her horse seems to be the winner of much of her time."

"I cannot fault her for that. I was much the same way with my mare. My governess always said if the horse won the battle for my time, I would be a positive Philistine in the drawing room." Closing her fan, Miranda smiled at the dowager countess.

The door to the room opened and the four gentlemen sauntered in, looking handsome in their evening clothes. Reginald's bright green attire cast the more traditional colours in the shade, but Miranda preferred the conservative dress of the earl.

The brandy seemed to have a mellowing effect upon the group. Miranda noted Cresswood smiled at Julian as they conversed. She hoped he was considering his brother's request. She warmed as the earl's gaze fell upon her and he nodded congenially. She hoped her cheeks were not pink.

Lady Cresswood rose and urged the company to find seats in the chairs which the servants had arranged around the piano during dinner. After the group was seated, the dowager countess requested Lady Maude to begin. Cresswood was sent to turn the pages for the chit.

Miranda found herself seated between Cousin Amelia and Mr. Chartley. That young man wore a pained expression upon his face as his mother boldly pushed Lady Esther into the seat on the other side of him. Mrs. Chartley pointedly stared at Miranda, but she ignored the matron's desire to sit beside her son. The man needed some space.

As the entertainment began with a country song performed by Lady Maude, Miranda languidly played with her fan. She watched the earl as he stood behind the pianist, following the music. As he leaned forward and turned the page for Lady Maude, the girl looked up at Cresswood with a simpering smile. Miranda turned away, for she felt a gnawing inside.

Needing something to occupy her she leaned close to the Tulip and whispered, "I understand you have brought a new carriage to Oakhill. It is said to be quite splendid."

The dandy's mood seemed suddenly buoyant. With a quick glance around at the group, he leaned over and said, "Yes, would you care to come to the carriage house on the m-morrow to see it? They delivered it just before I ran . . . I m-mean just before I left Town. I selected all the colours and m-materials for it m-myself."

"If you would be so kind as to help me walk to the stables I should love to see your carriage and mayhap walk in the garden later." Miranda continued to avert her gaze from the pair at the front of the group.

Mrs. Chartley, who'd found a chair at the end of the row, cleared her throat as she peered around the others at her son. Miranda sat back. She didn't want the young man to get a tongue lashing for talking during Lady Maude's lackluster performance.

After two unrecognizable tunes, Lady Maude surrendered the piano to her sister amid polite applause. Miranda's fingers tightened on her fan as she watched the girl thank the earl excessively for his assistance with her sheet music.

The younger sister chose another folk tune. She played with the same lack of skill as her sister. But where Lady Maude fluttered her eyes at the earl, Lady Esther kept hers locked intently on the sheet music.

Finally, Miranda's turn came. Mr. Chartley helped her to the piano, where the earl waited to turn the sheet music. Her heartbeat seemed so loud as she sat upon the bench; she was sure the earl could hear it.

As she got ready to play, the earl leaned down and said, "Ah, I see you play a Mozart concerto. Did my mother tell you I have a weakness for all classical music, Miss Hamilton?"

Miranda's heart fluttered as she looked up into the handsome face and noted a look of admiration in his eyes. "No, my lord, 'twas just an old favorite of mine. I hope you shall not be disappointed with the rendition."

The earl straightened and reached out to adjust the page. "I have faith you are up to the task. Little appears to be beyond your talents."

Miranda was surprised to see her hands did not tremble as she placed them upon the keys. Looking up at the sheet of music, she took a deep breath and began. It was an old familiar tune which she had played often for her mother. As her fingers moved fluidly over the keys, she was drawn into the beauty of the melody, forgetting about her nerves and worries but not about the masculine presence at her side.

Though Miranda tried to lose herself in the music, she remained conscious of the earl's strong hands turning the sheets for her. When she finished the piece, she put her hands in her lap as a moment of silence fell upon the chamber.

The drawing room suddenly filled with loud applause. She could hear several voices praising her playing, but the most important voice was the earl as he leaned forward to offer her his arm. He spoke softly, for her ears only. "Miss Hamilton, that was truly exceptional. You have a true talent. I very much hope you will consent to play for us another time.

A shock ran through her as she put her hand upon his arm and felt his strong muscles beneath the fabric. Cresswood's presence was intoxicating as he stood over her. His eyes locked with hers and seemed filled with a look of wonder and admiration.

As she rose, her knees wobbled unreliably. She felt dizzy with exhilaration as they stood before one another. The applause seemed far away. Suddenly Julian appeared beside the couple, breaking the magic spell which entwined them. She tore her gaze from the earl's handsome face and smiled weakly at his brother.

"Mary, you must let me help you back to your seat. Upon my word, you play divinely." Julian took her hand and placed it upon his sleeve as he led her away from his brother. Miranda felt the candles burned less bright and the room seemed cold as she left the earl's side.

Nine

It was almost noon when the carriage bowled swiftly up under the portico at Oakhill. Jumping lightly down, Cresswood handed the reins to the young groom who descended from the tiger perch. Striding through the main hall, he went directly to the library to restore the documents he had taken to Crawley to their proper place.

Distracted while discussing estate matters, Miss Hamilton now stole into the earl's thoughts. He was no closer to knowing the truth about her than when she arrived. But he was now more certain than not that she wasn't Peter's lightskirt. However, to his increasing chagrin, she seemed to become more enticing to him with each encounter.

Entering the library, the earl discovered Ellen sitting alone at a small table near the window, playing Patience with a bored expression. Upon seeing her brother, she dropped the cards in an untidy heap. "Were your business matters successfully accomplished?" She rose and came to the front of the desk, opposite to where Charles stood. Curiously, she eyed the documents he held.

"Yes," the earl said as he placed the papers inside his desk and closed the drawer. Looking up at Ellen, he queried, "Where are the others? You are rarely to be found alone in this house."

His eyebrows arched as she sat down in one of the chairs before the desk. Thinking she wished to speak to him of some matter, he took his seat.

She rolled her eyes theatrically before she answered, "Cousin Amelia convinced Mary to help her sort silks for her latest stitchery. She is now determined to make baby jackets for the foundling home. I feared they might want me to embroider a jacket, so I found an errand to take me from the room and never returned."

"I see. You would rather be sitting here bored than have a needle in your hands. That would be a fate worse than never being allowed to ride again," Cresswood teased as he sat back in his chair.

"Ha! There is no fate worse than never being able to ride again. But don't scold me. Mother and my governess have finally accepted I shall never excel in certain ladylike arts. Let us speak of you for a moment."

Suspicious, Cresswood observed his sister playing with the long yellow ribbons on her gown as she coyly watched him. He narrowed his eyes as he picked up the letter opener and languidly turned it over in his hand. "What, pray, do you wish to know?"

"Who is Lady Bronson?" Ellen asked with studied innocence.

The earl's hand froze, and the letter opener clattered to the desk. "I suppose I have Lady Maude and Lady Esther to thank for such an impertinent question. Those young ladies' minds dwell on rather inappropriate matters. Some like to bandy others' names about Town. As to Lady Bronson, she is an acquaintance of mine. I know many people in Town and I don't deem it necessary to inform my family of every one of them."

At his harsh tone, a rosy blush covered Ellen's face. His own neck felt hot. He did not wish his sister to know of his liaisons of that sort, and somehow the lady's name seemed tawdry upon the innocent girl's lips.

"I apologize, Charles. I did not mean to pry," Ellen sputtered out, the pink flush still upon her cheeks. "Lady Maude said you were being linked with the lady and I hoped we might wish you happy soon."

Pushing erect, the earl came round the desk to lean down next to his sister. Taking her hand, he gently squeezed it. "No, I apologize for being so harsh, little one. But you must be careful when you come to Town. There is always a great deal of gossip. Don't be drawn into such a vice."

"Yes, Charles." As Ellen looked up at him with a tremulous grin, the gong sounded for the midday meal.

"You go join the others. I must hurry and change. I am rather sharp set after driving to Crawley." Shooing his sister from the library, he hurried to his rooms, determined to be quite charming during the meal to make up for his harsh tone.

He arrived in the dining room a scant ten minutes after leaving his sister. The other members of the family and their guests were already present. Miss Hamilton looked lovely in a lilac muslin gown he recognized as one of his sister's. Her lips curved into a shy smile as he entered. His mouth answered of its own will.

Lady Cresswood informed the butler he could now serve as Cresswood pulled out his chair, making his apologies for being late. Miss Hamilton sat beside his brother. The earl overheard him say he'd just returned from the errand Charles sent him upon.

As Miller served the last of the soup, Cresswood questioned his brother about the morning trip. "Was the west field flooded?"

"No, the bailiff said the new dam is holding fine." Julian spooned up a mouthful of the hot chicken broth.

"Thank you for inspecting that field for me. I could not delay meeting with my man in Crawley this morning. But while I was in town, I learned there is to be a mill this afternoon, if you should like to take Reggie and go." Cresswood thought it was a diversion which would keep the boy amused and out of Miss Hamilton's orbit. While he didn't think the young lady a jade any longer, he still would not wish his brother to become attached at so young an age.

"I find prizefights to be barbarious events. It should sicken any gentlemen with pretensions to gentility," Aunt Agatha's strident voice proclaimed.

Cresswood glanced down the table at Reggie, understanding the implied command for her son to refrain from joining the expedition, but doubting his cousin's ability to perceive the hint.

Reggie's eyes were on his soup bowl, and he seemed more intent on his meal than the conversation.

"I believe man shall always be something of a barbarian, Aunt Agatha. We leave it to the ladies to keep that side of our nature subdued." Looking back to Reggie, Cresswood inquired, "Do you wish to go to a mill, Reggie?"

"What? A mill?" The dandy eyed the earl vaguely as

clear evidence he was not attending the conversation. "Barbarians to fight, you say?"

Allowing his spoon to drop into his bowl noisily, Julian responded, "Heavens, Reggie, do you want to go to a mill or not? Does it truly matter who will fight?"

Looking around at the smiling faces, Reggie answered, "In truth, I should much prefer seeing two prize-fighters spar instead of two barbarians. 'Twould have more style and less . . . savagery."

Grinding his teeth, Julian took a deep breath. "There will be no barbarians at the mill, only the local gentry and a simpleton . . . or two. Do you wish to join me or not?"

"Do you allow simpletons to run loose in the county?" Reginald asked as he sat back and patted his mouth with his napkin.

"Why not? We seem to allow them free reign in the manor," Julian quipped.

The earl heard his sister stifle a giggle as their aunt glared down the table. Frowning at his brother, he addressed his cousin. "Reggie, it is an ordinary mill. Do you wish to accompany Julian?"

"I cannot. I have promised to take Miss Hamilton out to the carriage house to inspect my new rig this afternoon and then for a walk in the gardens." The jest completely escaped the young man, as shown by his bland countenance.

"Don't be ridiculous, Reginald. What interest could Miss Hamilton have in viewing carriages?" Agatha Chartley stated as she eyed the girl in question. "If you must have some form of entertainment, then go to your mill. I shall not tease you about it."

Miss Hamilton, who the earl observed was quietly eating her soup, ignored Mrs. Chartley as she spoke. "Please go with Lord Julian, Mr. Chartley, for I might inspect your carriage on another occasion. I should not want to overdo on my first day out of doors."

"Don't worry about Mary, Reggie. *I* shall take her to the conservatory this afternoon and tell her the Benton family history," Ellen offered, smiling.

"Egad, not that," Julian teased. "You will be bored beyond belief, Mary, for the Bentons are a dull lot."

"I must say I find that a falsehood, sir. Neither you nor your brother appear to be dull," Miss Hamilton countered.

The earl watched Julian's pride swell as the boy went back to his soup. As he glanced down the table, his gaze met hers. Her expression looked open and honest, no hint of deceit or flummery. Reluctantly breaking the contact as he too went back to the meal, he worried about his brother's response to the compliment. It was just the thing to turn an impressionable young man's head.

Lady Cresswood said, "I think a quiet afternoon in the conservatory would be delightful. The young men can be off to Crawley and their entertainment. As for you, Mary, we have a family of domestic ducks which are quite entertaining to watch in the small pond. I know a country-bred girl like yourself will not think poorly of our pastoral amusements."

A smile curved the girl's lovely mouth as she turned easily towards his mother. "No, I should think not. I love the outdoors, Lady Cresswood."

The earl's gaze moved slowly down her lovely neck to the hint of creamy white shoulders. He barely noticed as the conversation moved on to other topics. A sudden desire to kiss the gentle curve of her neck caused him to shake himself out of his reverie. He was becoming more drawn to the girl with each passing day.

Cresswood realized he must put his suspicions to rest about the girl. He was torn with conflicting thoughts. When he was with her, she enchanted and intrigued him.

Searching his memory of the conversation with Peter, he looked for something which he might use to truly determine if she might be the swindler. Despite his mother's confidence, he felt uneasy about her for some strange reason.

As the talk of the day's activities continued at the table, his mind returned to the night he took Sir Peter to his town house. As he glanced at his brother, who was telling the family a tale from school, he remembered Peter mentioned a brother of the lady in question. A hardened gamester, his friend said. Where was the mysterious brother? Then he remembered Miss Hamilton's avowals to be an orphan. She had no brother.

Watching Miss Hamilton laugh at Julian's story, he resolved to put his suspicions about the lady aside for now. She showed no particular preference nor desire for either Reggie or Julian. Perhaps she was just what she claimed to be, a young woman trying to earn a living as a governess. With that thought, Charles set about enjoying his lunch.

Past its zenith, the sun nicely warmed the conservatory. Chairs were placed near the doors of the glass-enclosed room for the young ladies to enjoy the mild

November afternoon. The air was cool without being uncomfortable for the ladies in their pelisses and bonnets.

Ellen worked on a piece of embroidery with decidedly frayed edges. As the girl pierced the material with another sloppy stitch, she told Miranda an anecdote about another one of her cousins.

"Lavinia is mother to a darling baby boy named Perry. Her husband, Lord Worthing, holds a nice property in Berkshire. They met at Covent Garden during her first Season. Lilith, my other cousin, is in a delicate condition. Her husband is Lord Barwell, and they live near Bath. It was love the first time they beheld each for Lili and her baron. Do you believe in such, Mary?"

Turning away from watching a groom exercise a young horse in the distant stable yard, Miranda brought her attention back to Ellen. "My mother always declared it was thus with her and my father. I am not sure, though," she responded, as a pair of slate grey eyes and a charming smile came into her mind.

"I think it would be so romantic to know at once a gentleman is one's destiny." Ellen gazed into the distance. "To not have to bother with all that going to Town for a Season and such nonsense. What would be superb would be to fall in love at first sight with a gentleman who bred horses."

Miranda shook her head as she smiled at Ellen's continued desire to avoid a Season. "I would advise caution about such matters. History is full of young ladies who were deceived by a flashing smile and handsome looks. I have often heard you must look to how a man treats others to find his true worth, especially if one is an heiress."

Miranda adjusted the slipping quilt which Cousin Amelia insisted she drape over her legs and thought about the pain her own fortune had brought. If there were a way to give it to her stepbrother to leave her alone, she would.

Losing interest in stitching, Ellen dropped the hated embroidery hoop on her lap. "Yes, Mama warned me about the many amusing fellows in Town who can sometimes be fortune hunters. 'Tis quite frightening to think of being wanted only for your dowry."

"True, but it does not only happen to ladies. Think how it must be for your brother to have both title and fortune, and be pursued for only that reason." The faces of Lady Maude and Lady Esther rose in Miranda's mind as she spoke.

"Yes, I sometimes think Charles will never marry," Ellen mused.

Miranda felt disconcerted by the idea of the earl never marrying. Curiosity made her ask, "Why?"

"Mother declares she has introduced him to the most eligible young ladies over many Seasons and he was clearly bored by them all." Flushing, Ellen added, "I learned that he was linked to one lady, but it does not appear to be someone he would care for us to meet."

Miranda knew she referred to one of the questionable women of which she and Ellen should not be aware. Her mother spoke to her of such when she questioned old Lord Redford's many trips to Hastings. The idea of the earl with another woman sent a sharp pain through her chest, and she had to resist the urge to rub the ache.

A silence fell between the two girls as each sat lost in her own thoughts. A footfall sounded on the stone terrace behind them and a maid appeared. "Lady Ellen," she curtsied, "your mother wishes a moment of your time in her apartments."

"I shall return as quickly as I can, Mary. If you become chilled or tired before I come back, merely ring the bell on the table and one of the servants can help you inside." Ellen tossed her abused stitchery upon the nearby table, then left the terrace.

Sleepy, Miranda closed her eyes and sat enjoying the unseasonably comfortable afternoon. Her foot was rapidly improving and she must make a plan for leaving. But today she would merely enjoy the quiet. She still suffered occasional nightmares about her cold night in the hay.

Brisk footsteps crossing the stone terrace caused her to open her eyes. Lord Cresswood strode toward her from the direction of the stables. He came to her chair and smiled down at her.

"Good afternoon, Miss Hamilton."

How handsome he looked in his tan buckskin breeches and brown riding jacket. Miranda felt her composure was under attack as she stared into his face.

"Good afternoon, Lord Cresswood. Were you out enjoying this delightful weather?" She spoke with as steady a voice as she could manage. Her heart was misbehaving in the most ridiculous manner.

"No, I fear one of my tenants was injured this morning and I went to make certain the doctor was sent for, as well as a strong lad to take over his duties while he recovers."

"That was most kind of you, sir." She smiled gently.

"Not kind, Miss Hamilton, just a part of good management." The earl's gaze seemed to take in every aspect of her face. "Have they all abandoned you to your own devices?"

"Lady Ellen was here for a bit, but your mother had need of her. I was quite enjoying the quiet."

"Are you able to take a short stroll?" The earl looked down at her injured limb.

Delighted, Miranda said, "I think I might manage a short walk."

Lord Cresswood extended his arm to her. Miranda rose, placing the quilt on the vacated chair, and settled her hand on the offered limb, marveling at the muscular feel of the earl through the wool jacket.

"I thought to show you the pond and our little family of ducks."

The pair strolled at a leisurely pace down a stone path. Charles looked down at the woman who walked beside him. Curious, he inquired, "You seem too young and beautiful to be engaged as a governess, Miss Hamilton. I can think of few wives who would wish such a lady under the same roof as their husband. Have you been at it a long time?"

The lady looked up at him distrustfully, as if he were again prying into her history, but he returned her stare with no guile. He truly was curious, having put much of his suspicion aside.

"In truth, my lord, I was on my way to London to apply for my first post. Do you think it will be difficult for me to find a position?"

Charles suspected it would be impossible, but he didn't wish to tell Miss Hamilton the harsh truth about the world. Instead, he decided to make light of the matter. "Not if you apply with the right sort of family, say one where the mother is quite old . . . and blind . . . and lacking in her wits."

Miranda laughed. "You are being quite ridiculous, my lord."

"True. I should have said the father must be old and blind and lacking in his wits."

"I come to think you believe me only suited to teaching a family of lackwits. I would do better to apply directly to Bedlam."

"There you have it. The perfect job for a beautiful lady." Charles smiled down at the lovely upturned face. Then, growing a bit sober, he added, "I am sure, however, that my mother would be more than delighted to give you a character reference."

"That would be most kind, my lord."

The pair arrived at the pond. The mother duck and her nearly grown offspring came gliding across the glass-smooth water, hoping to get some treat from the couple by the water's edge.

"They are quite beautiful. They remind me of the ducks we had when I was younger."

The earl pulled a small pouch from his pocket and handed it to his companion. "I thought you might like to feed them."

"Thank you, my lord." Miranda took the pouch and poured the oats into her gloved palm. The family of ducks came waddling up the bank and crowded around the offered treat. She was pleased at how unafraid the little creatures were as she stooped to feed them.

"You look as if you have done this very often before."

"Oh, no, for my brother would never allow the waste

of grain for—" Miranda froze. She'd made a terrible blunder.

She dumped the remaining grain from the pouch onto the ground and the family of ducks crowded round. With trepidation, she stood and knew at once his lordship had withdrawn from her once again by the stone cold expression on his face.

"So, you have a brother, Miss Hamilton." His voice was cold and exact.

A faint thread of hysteria ran though her voice as she tried to explain to him. "He is my *step*brother, and I prefer not to notify him of my present location or situation. There is an estrangement between us, my lord."

"I understand he has a fondness for gaming." The earl's gaze remained riveted upon her face.

"Gaming?" As her mind swirled with fear and confusion, Miranda replied vaguely, "Yes, I believe he is often under the hatches. He wagers a good deal."

"And you are quite certain you do not wish to contact him?" the earl demanded.

"Quite sure, sir," she stated adamantly.

"Very well, Miss Hamilton."

Finally in control of her emotions, she glanced back at the earl. Now his eyes were shuttered, as if some door had permanently closed.

"I have just remembered some estate business I have to attend to, if you will excuse me." The earl hastily turned and walked back up the path to the house. The slamming of the door as he entered the manor sounded final.

Reeling from the encounter, Miranda knew she had no one to blame but herself. Her own loose tongue had caught her in a falsehood. He now knew she *did* have a relative. She could only thank God he didn't know her stepbrother's name.

An overpowering sense of despair assailed her. Tears welled in her eyes as she stood alone and alienated, knowing the earl again wished her gone from his estate. As the line of ducks finished with their dinner and paddled past, hot tears spilled down her cheeks.

The sound of a dried leaf crunching startled Miranda. Julian approached, but the smile left his face as he perceived her distress.

"Mary, what happened? Are you in pain? You should not walk such a great distance unassisted as yet." Julian put his arm around her shoulders in a brotherly fashion.

"I know it was foolish to walk so far, but the pond was so enchanting it lured me from the terrace. My ankle shall be fine if you will assist me back to the manor." Miranda gladly grasped the excuse for her crying, brushing the tears from her face as he helped her up the walk.

"Promise me you will not allow Reggie to talk you into going to the carriage house today. You must not overtire yourself or you will have a relapse." Julian tenderly held her to him as they slowly walked back up the path.

"I promise. I am surprised to find you back from Crawley so soon. Was the mill postponed?" Miranda smiled, attempting to be rid of her depressed mood.

"It turned out to be a rather tepid affair. Just some locals playing at prizefighting. Reggie and I are used to much better sport in London, so we agreed to return home. We did stop for drinks with some chaps from the neighborhood, but Reggie was soon bored, so here we are. He went to change, but I saw you by the pond and decided to join you. And very glad I did, for now I see you needed assistance." Julian steadied her as she took the first step of the terrace.

Miranda glanced up at the manor and detected a figure at the library window observing their progress. The earl stood rigidly behind the glass. Suddenly aware of Julian's arm round her shoulders, she managed the final step.

The black look upon the earl's face caused her to pull away from Julian slightly, and she felt her face flush red with embarrassment. After thanking him for his assistance, she sank tiredly into the chair, pulling the quilt up to warm her chilled heart as she still felt the earl's cold stare on her back.

What a fool he was, the earl thought. He sat before the small fire in the library drinking deeply of the brandy beside him. Miss Hamilton had lulled his suspicions about her to the point that he himself had fallen under her spell. He'd actually begun to think he was truly wrong about her and she was a governess, but his interview with her this afternoon confirmed she possessed a gamester brother and had lied about the matter. Along with the other coincidences of name and description, this new information was very damning, indeed.

Crossing one elegantly clad leg over the other, Cresswood continued his musings. Miss Hamilton's behavior in the garden with Julian this afternoon was the worst of it. No respectable young girl allowed a gentleman not her fiance to clutch her to him in such a manner. She might truly have designs upon Julian, but she must realize by now the boy was without funds until he reached his majority.

The earl stood up rather slowly and poked at the dying blaze with the iron at the side of the fireplace. As new flames leapt up, he settled back into his chair, refilled his glass from the nearly empty decanter, then took a drink as the door to the room swung open.

"Charles! I thought everyone had gone to bed." His mother held several books. A long grey braid hung from her nightcap, and she was dressed in nightgown and wrapper. Her gaze left his face to survey the decanter upon the table, then moved back to him. A crease appeared between her brows.

"Is there some problem, dearest?" She came forward and set the books down on the table edge, pulling her wrapper tightly around her as she gazed at him.

Remembering his manners, he rose unsteadily. "No, Mother, I was just worrying about . . . some of the problems on the estate."

She moved over to the opposite chair and took a seat. "Sit down before you fall down, Charles," she pronounced sternly.

Sinking into the seat, the earl watched his mother's worried face. Suddenly, he realized he needed to stop all his self-pity and accept the fact the girl was exactly what he'd suspected. "I apologize for my condition, Mother. I rarely indulge in brandy, but . . ." His voice trailed off. He had no excuse he wanted to share with his mother.

"Does this have something to do with Mary?" his mother asked perceptively.

"What would make you think Miss Hamilton is at the root of my drinking?" To avoid his mother's penetrating gaze, he looked into the fire.

"I may be merely a female, but I am not blind, Charles. You suspect Mary of some dark doings of which you will not tell me, and yet you find yourself attracted to her. I have observed your behavior around her. Is that not true?" The earl looked into his mother's sympathetic gaze.

Cresswood propelled himself from the chair and paced the room. "You seem determined to fancy a romance between myself and Miss Hamilton. I, on the other hand, worry about Julian and the effect this woman might have upon him. Or even upon Reginald."

"I think you are worried about your brother and cousin simply because she affects you so greatly. Julian's manner may be overfamiliar with Mary not from strong emotion but because he sees her as a sister. As to Reggie, he is Agatha's worry. You refine too much upon the matter." His mother rose.

"I think what worries you the most in this situation is that Mary represents a new responsibility to you," she said as she shelved the books. "I would guess you think you have had your fill of being in charge of others, but I assure you a wife is very different from siblings." His mother selected a new book and thumbed through it.

After giving a mirthless laugh, the earl snorted, "Mother, you read too many romance novels. They make you believe in love in the oddest of circumstances. Well, I can assure you I know too much of Miss Hamilton's past to fall prey to her charms."

"Then you have acquired confirmation of your suspicions?" Lady Cresswood looked back at him with a frown.

"No." The earl stopped abruptly, his head swirling from the brandy. He reached out to the mantel to steady himself as his mother walked towards the door.

"Then do not say you know of her background, for all you know for sure is Julian brought a young lady to the manor who behaves with manners and breeding. I am tired of trying to convince you that you have misread this situation, but I believe there is a saying that none are so blind as those who will not see. Now, I shall go to bed and recommend you do the same, for you are beginning to look quite foxed." She closed the door with a snap.

Angrily, he dropped into his chair. She'd spoken as if he were some lovesick mooncalf. It was ridiculous to think he was in love with a woman who was little better than a . . . felon.

Struggling to his feet, he determined he must go to bed. All was beyond his mental capacities tonight. One thing he was certain of: his brother might not appreciate it, but until the chit was gone, the earl meant to be his constant companion.

Ten

Pulling a green silk thread from the riot of colours upon her lap, Miranda placed the strand in the small basket beside her while the warm afternoon sun poured through the casement windows. Scanning the array of colours, her mind was on the earl as she distractedly wondered which shade to separate next. Cousin Amelia interrupted her daydreaming.

"Mary, you know 'tis not necessary for you to remain with me doing this dull work. You could go with Lady Cresswood and Ellen to visit some of their local friends," Mrs. Warren offered as she pulled the needle through a tiny jacket.

"Oh, I don't feel quite ready to be out visiting as yet," Miranda insisted. She couldn't be certain Sylvester remained in the area, and it would be disastrous to accidently meet him upon the road. A chill ran down her spine at the thought. "Besides, Mr. Chartley is coming soon to take me to see his new carriage and I should dislike disappointing him, for he seems excited to have someone take an interest."

"Well, don't be surprised if that young man does not come, for I saw his mother speaking with him after nuncheon. She keeps him very much under her thumb.

I fear she cannot bring herself to realize he is a man." Cousin Amelia put her sewing down, and solemnly added, "He's such a dear, but I suspect Mr. Chartley lacks the strength of character to assert himself with her."

Silence fell between the women as each continued with her own task. Miranda's thoughts dwelled on the earl. He again treated her as if she weren't fit to sit in the same room with his family. A heaviness centered around her heart.

Miranda looked up at the sound of the door opening. She smiled as Mr. Chartley entered with a definite strut. Pale grey buckskins encased his thin legs, and a lavender kerseymere coat covered a yellow and white striped waistcoat. He paused to survey the ladies through his quizzing glass.

She noticed no fewer than four fobs dangled from beneath the satin vest. His neck cloth was tied in an intricate manner that Miranda suspected must have a name.

"Good afternoon, ladies. You are both looking lovely today," he said, bowing with a flourish.

Miranda smiled at the young man. "Good afternoon, Mr. Chartley. I fear you cast us both in the shade, sir."

"I should never do anything as ungentlemanly as that." Reggie smoothed his waistcoat, smiling with pleasure at the compliment.

Looking up from her stitching, Cousin Amelia said, "You are a true Pink of the *ton,* dear boy. 'Tis always a delight when you visit us. You bring such an air of Bond Street with you."

"Thank you, Mrs. Warren," Reggie beamed. "Do you

care to join M-Miss Hamilton and m-me for a stroll to the carriage house?"

"No, you young people run along. I have a great deal too much work here for an outing. Besides, 'tis decidedly cooler today than yesterday. I don't enjoy being outdoors during the winter." The grey-haired lady returned to her work after she gestured them along.

"Then, if you are ready, M-Miss Hamilton?" Reginald leaned towards Miranda.

Placing her hand on the offered arm, she rose and allowed him to lead her into the hall. Miller stood ready with a borrowed blue pelisse and the new black bonnet. Thanking him, she donned the garment over the fashionable pink dress Ellen had loaned her and tied the ribbon of the hat.

A footman held a dark grey greatcoat with large yellow buttons for the baronet. The young man seemed to gain a measure of confidence from his dashing attire.

Exiting through the front doors, Miranda eagerly looked around while her companion enthused about his carriage. It was her first glimpse of Oakhill Manor from the outside, since she'd been in no state to admire the structure on her arrival. The facade was beautiful and elegant, definitely Elizabethan. She could understand the earl's pride in owning such a place.

As they rounded the corner, Miranda started when a window on the second floor flew open. Agatha Chartley's face appeared in the opening, the lace on her white cap fluttering in the breeze as she called, "Reginald, I wish to see you in my chambers in twenty minutes. Make certain you don't dawdle too long in the carriage house, young man."

Miranda watched as the animation left the dandy's face, replaced by a pink flush. Feeling sorry for the young man, she guessed at the struggle taking place within him.

When she glanced up at Mrs. Chartley, the hostile stare Miranda received shocked her. With a slight toss of the lady's head, the unfriendly face disappeared from the window. She obviously thought Miranda pursued her son.

"I know you m-must be disappointed in m-me for not being able to take your advice," Reggie stuttered as his flush deepened.

"I am not, sir. I know what it is to have such a parent, for my late stepfather was equally . . . overpowering. I would never judge anyone in such a situation. Just know your cousins are behind you, and when the time is right for you to assert yourself, you will know it." Miranda encouraged him with a smile.

"You know, M-Miss Hamilton, I come to think you are quite the nicest lady of my acquaintance. I should very m-much like to call on you once you are settled in Town." He led her towards the carriage house, entirely unaware of the inappropriateness of his request.

With a feeling somewhere between amusement and alarm, Miranda struggled to find an answer. "You realize of course, sir, I shall be employed as a governess in London. Even the best of employers might frown upon my receiving a gentleman visitor."

Before Reginald could respond, a shout from the stables drew their attention. Julian strode towards them with Cresswood close behind. "Good afternoon. May we join you?"

"Afternoon, Cresswood, Julian. I should be delighted for you to join us. We are on our way to the carriage house." Reggie's face glowed with pleasure at the added company.

Miranda searched the earl's face for some sign of welcome. A mask of cold dignity greeted her. A reserved "Miss Hamilton," along with a curt nod of his head, was all she received. As a sinking sensation rushed through her, she kept her features deceptively composed.

"Good," Julian said, falling into step with Reginald to question him about the carriage.

Miranda, aware of the earl's presence behind their party, heard the crunch of his boots on the path. He made no effort to join the conversation.

As they stepped into the carriage house, Reggie was rhapsodizing over his carriage. "I used only the colours lavender and yellow throughout my coach. I am looking for a team of m-matched white horses to pull it. Where did you get that m-magnificent set of bloods I saw in the stables, Cresswood?"

"From a fellow at Newmarket who needed some quick blunt. I don't recommend such a method, however. Have you tried Tattersall's?" the earl asked as he ran his eyes over the gleaming pastel coach with yellow trim.

"Yes, but they carried nothing to pique my interest the last time I went. I shall try again once I return to Town." The dandy ran his hand proudly over the lacquered paint, which was polished to a high luster.

"Well, Reggie, I must say 'tis quite impressive despite the colour, but how does it ride?" Cresswood asked as he stooped down to look under the vehicle.

Miranda gazed at the coach with little knowledge of

carriages. It looked lovely, with its pale lavender paint and yellow trim around the windows, door, and roof. Bright yellow wheels added to its sporty appearance. Brass fittings and two large brass lanterns at the front adorned the vehicle. In the window hung a yellow and white striped curtain with yellow fringe and tassel. To her untrained eyes, it looked impressive.

"Excellent suspension. It goes over cobblestones in Town like they were as smooth as a tabletop." Reggie walked to the back of the carriage.

Julian stepped up to stand beside Miranda. "I must say it is an impressive coach, if you must own a traveling carriage." He begrudgingly owned, then whispered to Miranda in an undertone, "I don't like the colour one bit. And *I* would never drive so staid a vehicle, for I enjoy something far sportier."

Smiling, Miranda whispered back, "His groom must have to polish it after each short trip to keep the dirt from ruining that lovely yellow colour."

Julian smiled. "True, but that would weigh little with a Tulip like Reggie."

Glancing up, she found the earl's cold stare upon them. Feeling uncomfortable under his grim scrutiny, Miranda moved away from Julian.

Reggie gestured for the group to come to the carriage door. "You must see the interior, for it is done in yellow satin and velvet."

As the dandy opened the door, Miranda limped forward to politely view the inside. Tired of the earl's unfriendly stare, she wished nothing more than to be back doing her dull job with Cousin Amelia.

The two brothers lingered at the front of the coach as

the earl drew Julian's attention to some point of interest. Miranda suspected Cresswood merely wished to keep the young man from her side, as if she might do him some harm.

Suddenly a strange sound emanated from Reggie as she came to his side. Miranda thought him choking. His body went rigid; then slowly he began to turn towards her. His face was completely ashen and his eyes looked unfocused during that brief moment. Then he fell forward, causing Miranda to jump to the side even as she attempted to catch his falling body.

"Cresswood!" Miranda called, as Reggie fell through her hands to the dirt-covered floor. The impact sent swirls of dust wafting up. Struggling to maintain her own balance and keep the weight off her still healing foot, she grabbed the open carriage door for fear she would fall as well.

"What happened?" the earl asked as he came and knelt over his cousin.

"I don't know. He was fine; then suddenly he looked ill and fell," Miranda answered with dismay.

The earl turned his cousin over on his back as Julian looked on with concern. The knot in his cousin's intricate cravat resisted Cresswood's efforts to untie it and help Reggie breathe. The earl swore softly.

A layer of dust covered Reggie from his neatly groomed hair to his once shiny boots. His face looked ghostly pale under the grime.

Still clutching the coach door, Miranda turned as a movement caught her eye from inside the darkened vehicle. Peering into the interior, her heart jumped. A hairy creature stared back at her. As the men discussed what troubled Reggie, she suddenly comprehended what she saw.

"Julian, I believe the answer to your cousin's problem is here." Miranda barely suppressed a smile.

The young man stepped around his brother and supine cousin to join her at the carriage door. With a shout of laughter, Julian said, "Why, he's only fainted!"

Standing, the earl frowned at the pair. "What?"

Miranda said, "I believe the discovery his new carriage is a nursery for Ruby and her new litter is more than he could handle." She reached to pat the red dog on the head before picking up a tiny squeaking pup, its eyes still closed.

Cresswood stepped up and eyed the red pup. "I suspect we shall find a rather large hole dug in the stall where Ruby was locked. Eh, girl?"

The dog's tail beat delightedly against the floor of the carriage as the earl spoke to her.

"But how the devil did she manage to get in Reggie's carriage?" Julian asked.

Miranda pointed to the open communicating door on the roof of the carriage. "Do you suppose Mr. Chartley will discharge his coachman for having left it open?"

Her pulse skittered alarmingly as the earl leaned close to her to gaze into the door at the carriage roof.

"No, Wiggins has been with the family for years. I would guess the size of the roof door was Reggie's own design. He repeatedly said he oversaw its construction closely. But we could spare his man a scolding if we can undo this situation before any further damage is done. I think we must get the dog and her litter moved immediately and set the maids to cleaning the dirt from

the seats. However, we must first revive Reggie." The
earl looked back at his dust-covered cousin. A gentle
smile tugged at his lips.

"There is a pail of water near the rear of the stables.
Shall I get it and douse him?" Julian asked with a devilish glint in his eyes.

"We might throw him in the pond as well, but I think
there are less drastic methods of reviving him. We don't
want to give him a fatal chill. Go get the grooms and
we shall carry him to the manor. I believe Cousin
Amelia can do something which will bring him around."

The earl smiled at Miranda for the first time that day
as Julian left them. "I fear we are in for a rare trimming
from Aunt Agatha."

Miranda felt a warmth flood through her as she gazed
up at his handsome countenance. "She must know you
did your best to keep Ruby contained in the stable, for
I heard your mother ask Julian about it in your aunt's
presence."

In a spontaneous gesture Miranda placed her hand on
his arm. She trembled as a frisson ran up her arm at the
feel of him through the fabric.

"Aunt Agatha is not reasonable when it comes to Reggie and his welfare." The earl gazed down at her, studying her with deep intensity.

Feeling unable to respond as his nearness nonplussed
her, she took a step back to get her emotions in hand.
Inadvertently, her foot caught on Reggie's sprawled boot,
causing her to lose her balance. She began to fall backwards.

With a fluid movement, the earl prevented her from
toppling. His strong hands sent strange sensations

through her as he clutched her waist and drew her back to him. She trembled with excitement at his touch even through her thick layers of clothing.

Cresswood's expression stilled as they stood face to face with his hands still resting at her waist. Miranda's heart pounded so strongly she thought she would faint. His eyes dropped to her lips and she sensed he would kiss her. Tilting her face up toward him, she eagerly waited.

The sound of Julian and the grooms approaching startled the entwined pair. The earl suddenly released her, managing little more than a hoarsely whispered, "Excuse me."

Turning to speak to the grooms, the earl moved away from Miranda as she steadied herself on the carriage door. With a deep ache in her heart, she watched his rigid back. She sensed he regretted his momentary lapse of formality. Watching him move to allow the grooms access to his cousin, her heart sank to see his cold mask firmly back in place.

Standing with his back to the drawing room windows, Cresswood watched the ladies surrounding his conscious but dazed cousin. Aunt Agatha paced, ranting about her son's state, leaving the earl disgusted with his aunt for her hysterics over Reggie but mostly with himself for his behavior with Miss Hamilton.

For all his determination to dismiss the chit from his mind, she'd sent his senses reeling as he'd kept her from falling in the carriage house. When he held her close and gazed into the clear blue eyes, he was overwhelmed with the desire to kiss her tantalizing mouth. It was madness.

His aunt's angry voice brought his thoughts back to the present. "I cannot believe you continue to allow Julian to keep that disgusting beast around when you know what a delicate constitution Reginald has." Mrs. Chartley paced before the sofa where her son lay.

Cousin Amelia worked at undoing the buttons at the top of Reggie's shirt. Nearly everyone in the room stared in amazement when the lady came to Julian's defense. "There is no harm in Ruby. Why, she is the healthiest animal I have ever seen. If Mr. Chartley falls ill, there is no one to blame but himself for lying around in the dust."

Julian hovered at Miss Hamilton's side as the lady attempted to wipe dust from Mr. Chartley's face. He completely ignored his aunt's tirade, but stared at Mrs. Warren as if she'd just announced plans to run naked through the gardens. To the earl's chagrin, Julian exchanged muted conversation with Miss Hamilton, and then the pair laughed.

Looking at his brother's innocent face, Cresswood knew he must get Julian away immediately. The boy would not be able to resist so lovely a charmer if he himself couldn't. The earl would make the arrangements today despite his promise to allow the boy to remain until Miss Hamilton was fully recovered.

Bringing his mind to bear on the present situation, he decided to first calm his aunt. She was slowly working herself into a state of near hysteria.

"Aunt Agatha, calm down." She stopped pacing to face him with a flushed countenance. "Might I remind you Reggie is a grown man and will come to no harm due to a simple swoon. As to the dog, she is an old family pet, and I would guess little harm occurred in the carriage which cannot be cleaned or replaced. I believe it simply took Reggie by surprise to see the pups in his prized vehicle."

Cousin Amelia waved burned feathers under Reggie's nose as the earl spoke. Tossing his head back and forth to avoid the pungent odor, Reggie pushed the feathers away with a dust-coated hand.

"Well, as to him coming to no harm, you can be certain I shall take him home immediately to insure that," Aunt Agatha snapped. "I cannot believe you would all behave so callously about my son's health. I am very disappointed in you, Cresswood. You encouraged Reginald to charge round the countryside. And Julian dragged him to that horrid mill with all the low types one finds at such events. As for Miss Hamilton, she seems to have her own reasons for luring my son to the cold stables."

During her speech, Julian's face became outraged, Cousin Amelia looked frightened, and Miss Hamilton sat with her mouth parted in shock.

Losing his own temper, the earl protested, "Aunt Agatha—"

"Mother!"

Silence fell upon the room with the one word uttered loudly and with no stuttering by Reginald. "You will apologize to my cousins and Miss Hamilton at once. I am not some foolish lad led astray by anyone. I am a grown man and I make my own decisions."

Everyone stared at the dandy's grimy face as he

perched on one elbow. His assertive pronouncement left all but his mother speechless.

"Apologize? You don't know what you are saying. Lie down, for you shall do yourself a harm by trying to rise and I will—"

"No, Mother, I want you to apologize now." Reginald struggled to sit up fully, then narrowed his eyes as he glared at his mother with grim countenance.

Cresswood never before saw such a determined look on the delicate young man's face. It was as if a man replaced the foppish boy before his very eyes.

Agatha Chartley stared at her son for a few minutes in stunned silence. Seeing something new in her son's countenance, she turned to the earl. "I am sorry if I spoke too harshly, Cresswood. A mother's natural concern for her child can make her say unkind things when emotionally distraught. You must realize that I know you and Julian would never do anything to harm my Reginald."

"I completely understand, Aunt," Cresswood said, curious to see what Reggie would do next.

"And Miss Hamilton, Mother," Reginald ordered.

The earl saw his aunt's hands clench into fists before she turned to the girl, with thinned lips. "I am sorry if I offended you, Miss Hamilton." There was little apology in Aunt Agatha's tone.

"Think nothing of it, Mrs. Chartley. I know your distress at seeing your son in such a condition was great."

"Yes, that is quite true." Agatha glanced back at her son.

"Well, Mother, I believe you can now accompany me to my room, for I must change." Reginald glanced down at his soiled clothes with distaste. "I fear we may need those feathers once Gresham sees my attire, poor fellow."

"Gresham? Who cares—" Mrs. Chartley intoned, then sputtered out after a quelling look from her son.

"Mother, your arm please. We shall discuss whether we return to Town or go to my estate." Reginald rose shakily but with a confident manner.

"Would you like a footman to assist you, Reggie?" The earl watched his cousin walk unsteadily with his mother towards the door.

"No, I shall be fine. Mother and I shall see you at dinner," Reggie spoke crisply.

"Good heavens, I never expected that young man to ever stand up to his mother," Cousin Amelia said with surprise after the door closed behind the departing pair.

"I daresay we are all full of unknown depths." When the earl looked at Miss Hamilton, her face held a bemused smile. He could feel himself drawn to her even now. He must take action immediately.

"Julian, I need to speak with you in the library for a few moments. If you ladies will excuse us." The earl strode purposefully from the room.

Several minutes later in the library, the earl sat looking at his brother across the desk. "I must send you to Southampton."

"Southampton? Whatever for?" Julian looked puzzled.

"My yacht is there being refitted." The earl picked up a crystal paperweight, avoiding his brother's piercing stare.

"I don't understand. What can that have to do with me? I know nothing about your boat."

"The captain wants someone to come down and approve all the changes being made, and I am unable to go now." The earl rolled the crystal over, pretending a vast interest in the object.

"But I don't know anything about your changes. I wouldn't be able to say if they are right. Besides, I don't wish to leave until Mary is completely well and on her way," Julian argued.

"You needn't worry about Miss Hamilton," the earl practically shouted. Clenching the crystal in his hand, he continued in a quieter tone. "I must have someone go and *I* shall make certain the lady is taken to her destination in London."

"But, Charles, I—"

"This is not a request, Julian. I must have you in Southampton as soon as possible."

Rising with a definite scowl, Julian angrily stated, "This is a fool's errand, for I know nothing about the business."

"You will go all the same," the earl said. His voice forbade further argument.

With one last angry glance at his brother, Julian went to the door. "It would seem I have little choice."

The library door slammed. He felt guilty for forcing Julian to go against his will, but he wanted his brother safely away from that beguiling girl. He sat back and closed his tired eyes, but beautiful blue eyes and golden hair drifted into his thoughts. Blast, he thought as he opened his eyes and pulled a ledger to him. Could he find no peace?

* * *

The setting sun beat down upon Miranda as she sat on the marble bench near the terrace steps. A chilly hint of rain from the gathering clouds on the horizon made the warm rays pleasant. Staring out at the deep green pond, she tried to clear her thoughts of the earl and her wanton behavior in the carriage house. She lost all sense of propriety when in his presence.

A brisk breeze brushed her face as she watched the family of ducks drift across the pond, heading for their nest. She must find a home as well. Glancing down at her gloved hands, she clenched them as the thought sent a nervous spasm through her. Her foot was better. She needed to go before the earl asked any questions about the brother she'd denied having.

Miranda felt a scream of frustration hovering at the back of her throat. She must leave Oakhill and soon. She must slip away in a manner in which the Bentons would never be able to tell her stepbrother where she had gone should they learn her true identity.

With resolution, she sorted through various ways of slipping away. As she searched her mind for the best plan, she heard someone approaching.

Julian came around the corner of the building, striding for the stables. Angrily slapping his crop upon his boots, he walked towards her, muttering.

"Mary, you will not believe it. Cresswood *ordered* me to Southampton." Julian paced the stone walk.

"Why?" Miranda asked, already knowing the answer. The earl saw her as some kind of threat to his brother.

"Oh, he gave some ridiculous excuse, but it is just one more opportunity to make me do his bidding." Julian fumed. "He shall never treat me as an equal. I wasted my time trying to get him to allow me a little freedom from his yoke."

"I think you misjudge his reasons." Miranda didn't want to be the cause of discord between the brothers.

"Well, if I do, it runs in the family." Julian continued slapping his boots with the crop as he paced. "I think I will refuse to go. I will go to London instead."

As Miranda watched Julian rage against his brother, it slowly dawned upon her he could help her and wouldn't betray what he knew to his family, at least until she was safely away. If he truly intended to go to Town, he could take her.

"Julian, I wish to tell you something very important." She gestured to the bench. "Will you join me?"

He halted and eyed her suspiciously. She knew he suspected she might try to talk him out of defying his brother.

Reaching up she took his gloved hand. " 'Tis not what you think at all. I want to tell you the truth about myself."

"Truth?" he asked, raising his dark eyebrows.

Miranda could see she'd gained his full attention. He came forward and sat down. Facing him, she began at the beginning. "My name is not Mary Hamilton."

"But we found your name in your case," Julian argued.

"No, that is the name of my governess, with whom I was going to stay while I searched for a position."

"But your brushes have the monogram of M and H. Cousin Amelia said so."

"That is because my name is Miranda Henley. Lady

Miranda Henley, to be exact." A sense of relief flowed through her as she spoke her own name again.

"Then why not tell us we made a mistake? Why the deception?" Julian looked offended as he drew his hand away from hers.

"That is what I am doing now. However, before I begin, you must promise me you will not reveal what I will tell you, especially to your family." Miranda looked deeply into Julian's eyes, searching for the answer she wanted.

"Why?" Julian asked doubtfully.

"Because by law they would have to surrender me to my guardian, were they to know the truth. Do you promise?"

Julian's eyes scanned her fearful face. Then he smiled reassuringly. Taking her gloved hand again, he said, "I promise."

Eleven

Though he struggled to make sense of the numbers in the ledger, Cresswood's mind refused to cooperate. After some twenty minutes of attempting to total two columns, he pushed the ledger aside with frustration and rose to pace.

At the library window, he froze. There in the garden sat Julian and Miss Hamilton, heads nearly touching as they spoke, hands entwined. Each gazed intently at the other as they conversed.

Raw emotion surged through Cresswood as he gazed at the pair, some primitive feeling he couldn't identify. He only knew he would like to strangle his own brother. No, he meant Miss Hamilton. Running his hands through his hair, he realized he didn't know what he meant, only that he must act.

Yanking the door open, he stepped onto the terrace, his thoughts in a turmoil. Striding purposefully towards the pair, he realized they were unaware of his approach, so intent was the conversation.

In a black rage, the earl came around and stopped before the couple, his arms rigid. He feared he might grab his brother to remove him from the girl's side if he relaxed them. What madness possessed him?

"Charles." Julian started, dropping the girl's hand as the earl coldly examined the couple.

Two pairs of guilty eyes stared at Cresswood. "I believe you should be packing for your trip. I expect you to be on the road before dawn in the morning." The earl spoke through clenched teeth.

Julian scanned his brother's unyielding face, then answered with a surprisingly docile, "Yes, whatever you wish, Cresswood."

Some secret communication seemed to pass between the twosome on the bench as they glanced at one another. Then Julian stood and walked back to the manor. The earl suspected something was afoot. He determined to watch his brother closely until he was safely away.

Miss Hamilton rose, her hands nervously clasped before her. He put his hand out to stop her departure, then drew back as if he'd touched a flame when his fingers brushed the shoulder of her pelisse.

Marshalling his anger, his voice dripped with sarcasm. "Miss Hamilton, may I ask you one question?"

"Yes, Lord Cresswood." She stood motionless before him, as if caught in a trap.

Her slender body inflamed him even as he spoke so rudely. "I am puzzled that a woman of your profession would spend so much time with an inexperienced pup like Julian. He shall have no income to speak of until he is five and twenty and even then I shall control much of that." With no positive proof at all, he'd accused her.

A frown drew her lovely brows together as the earl continued. *"I* am the one who can fulfill your every wish." Grasping her wrist, he suddenly drew her roughly to him. Her body arched provocatively as his arms surrounded her waist. Wide eyes stared at his, startled but not frightened.

The blood seemed to pound in his ears as he held her. Searching her face, he saw only lips parted invitingly. All caution left as he covered her lovely mouth with his own.

He'd intended a cool ravishment of her mouth, but harsh though the kiss began, it slowly softened, sending waves of desire through him. He no longer wanted to punish her for what she was, only to possess her. He felt her own response, tentative at first, then stronger as the kiss gentled.

As his passion rose, the sudden pressure of her hands pushing on his chest caused him to release her.

Lurching backwards as he freed her from the embrace, she drew her hands to her mouth. She stood rigidly proud, but her eyes reflected confusion. Breathlessly she uttered, "How dare you, sir?"

The words pierced his emotion-fogged brain like a dagger. What had made him behave so boorishly? As he searched his heart for the answer, his gaze traced a path over her pale face encircled by the black bonnet. He detected a slight tremble to her lovely lips, a hint of unshed tears glistening in her eyes.

Picking up her skirts, the lady suddenly darted away from him, the limp hindering her movement very little. He reached out to stop her, but realized he knew not what to say.

Lowering his hand, he stared desolately out at the pond as a cold wind whipped around him. His mind swirled with a mixture of desire for the chit and repulsion at his behavior. He'd behaved like a cad to a guest in his home. She drove him to distraction, but that excuse was insupportable.

The sound of the manor door slamming brought him back to his senses. Glancing around as if surprised to find himself still in the garden, he rubbed his hand over his face to clear his head. He walked briskly to the stables and shouted for the head groom. "I need my horse at once, Cuthbert."

With a flurry of activity, the black gelding appeared saddled and ready in a matter of minutes. The earl mounted and galloped out of the stable yard with a sense of purpose, leaving the whispering grooms behind.

Some time later, the earl pulled the animal back to a walk as he felt the horse's labored efforts to maintain the brutal pace. Cursing his thoughtlessness, he patted the highbred creature's neck. "I apologize, Mercury, for taking my frustrations out on you. I shall demand a second ration of oats for you, boy."

The horse twitched his ears at the sound of Cresswood's voice and slowly walked across the field as the earl tried to sort out his feelings. His main worry about his brother would be gone with Julian in the morning. But what about the girl? There was little doubt she was Sir Peter's ladybird after Cresswood learned she'd lied to him. Could he trust himself around her?

Cresswood knew her to be a practiced charmer. Women of her stamp excelled at such arts. She'd proven it with Peter and now again here at Oakhill. Nevertheless, the earl had thought himself above falling prey to such women. With a mirthless laugh, he realized she'd almost achieved her goal of bewitching him.

Cresswood stopped his horse at the creek which bordered his estate and allowed the animal to drink while he tried not to think about an enchantingly beautiful face. He would merely avoid her for the few remaining days she would be in his home. Once he dropped her at her address in Town, he'd notify Peter she was back and leave the matter to his friend. He would never have to see or think about Miss Mary Hamilton again.

Closing the door gently, Miranda stood leaning against the oak panel. She needed to be alone. She'd expected to find solace in her room, but Sally stood at the fireplace, starting at her sudden entrance.

"Miss Hamilton, you're early to change for dinner. Which dress shall it be?" Sally replaced the iron beside the fireplace as she finished stoking the fire. " 'Tis getting cold out. Jamie says there's rain a-comin'. Seems to always get colder after a good rain. We'll be havin' snow again afore you can say Jack Frost."

Bringing her hand up to cover her teary eyes, Miranda interrupted the maid's chatter. "Sally, I believe I shan't go down to dinner this evening. I have the headache. Do you think you could inform Lady Cresswood for me?"

"There now, Miss Hamilton, you let me get you out of that gown and into this nice warm bed. We'll have you feeling the thin' in no time a'tall." The maid came forward and fussed over her as Miranda struggled to hold back tears.

Some time later, she lay shivering under the covers, her mind on the scene in the garden. The earl had spoken to her with such disdain. She tried to swallow the lump that rose in her throat as his words came back to her. *I am the one who can fulfill your every wish.*

If only the words hadn't been spoken with such bitterness. He'd kissed her. The kiss was unbelievably intoxicating, and it finally opened her eyes to what she'd been afraid to admit to herself. She was in love. She knew she should be elated, but because she loved a man who held her in contempt, she felt more miserable than ever before in her life.

Tugging the blankets up around her neck, Miranda thought it ironic that the one thing she *must* do was leave Oakhill when the thing she wanted *most* was to stay. But she knew in her heart he only envisioned her as his mistress. He'd practically called her a lightskirt in the garden. Had a simple falsehood so convinced him of her low character? There seemed to be no way out of her situation but to go.

With this dismal thought, the tears rolled down her cheeks. She would never be with the man she loved. She felt almost a physical pain within her while the tears flowed freely until she fell into an exhausted sleep.

Miranda started awake some time later. The room was in darkness, except for the fire. Realizing she'd been asleep, she wondered about the time. As she turned over in bed, a figure rose from a chair near the window.

"Miss Hamilton, are you feeling better?" The maid came to the bed, pausing to light several candles on the bedside table.

"Sally, you startled me. Yes, thank you. Did you inform Lady Cresswood I was unwell?"

"Yes, Miss. She was quite worried, but I assured her it was just a headache and you only needed a little rest.

She said she'd come up later to see how you're doin'. If you're hungry, I'll run down and brin' up a little somethin' Cook made for you." The maid smiled hopefully.

Food held no enticement, but Miranda knew she must keep up her strength for the trip to Town. "That would be lovely, Sally."

As the door closed behind the maid, Miranda sat up to see the clock on the mantel. It showed half past nine. Sinking back into the warm covers, she wondered where the family was. Probably in the drawing room having tea. She imagined the warm glow of the candles reflecting on Cresswood's black hair as he bent to speak to someone. Shaking her head, she pushed the thoughts of the earl from her mind. It was useless dreaming.

Rubbing her dry, scratchy eyes, Miranda hoped Julian would get her a message before he retired. Would he really defy his brother and take her to Town? In her heart she hoped he wouldn't, but her mind told her she must go.

After she ate the soup and cold chicken Sally brought, she dismissed the maid for the evening, assuring her she would soon be asleep after Lady Cresswood's visit. Lying in the large bed, she stared at the ceiling as the clock slowly ticked away the minutes until she would leave the manor.

Some time later, Miranda heard voices in the hallway. After a knock, the dowager countess, Ellen, and Amelia Warren entered her room.

"Well, my dear, is your headache gone? Did your nap help?" Cousin Amelia asked anxiously as the trio came up to Miranda's bed.

"Yes, I am feeling much better." Miranda attempted

a wan smile as she noticed how closely Lady Cresswood observed her.

"We should not have let you start going into the garden so soon," Lady Ellen stated. "I know it's difficult to remain inside when the weather is nice, but I intend to make certain you don't go out tomorrow. I feel guilty for encouraging you to be in the open air the past few days."

Smiling at the dark-haired girl, Miranda responded, "But it was I who wanted to be up and moving. It was only a slight headache, so don't worry. I shall be fine."

The dowager countess worriedly scanned Miranda's face as if looking for some sign of illness. "I am sure you will, my dear, but if you would like Dr. Mason to come tomorrow, we can send for him. We want you to get well."

"I assure you I am much better. Please don't make a fuss, for it was only a trifle. I shall be more the thing in the morning," Miranda reassured the ladies.

"Then we will leave you to your much-needed rest." The dowager countess signaled the ladies to leave. "Good night, my dear."

"Good night, ladies, and thank you for everything." Miranda was relieved when the door closed behind the women. She felt guilty knowing she might be gone without a word of farewell.

Getting out of bed, she went to the small desk in the corner, taking the candle with her. Finding a quill and paper she quickly wrote a vague note to Lady Cresswood explaining she must leave and thanking her and her family for all their care. She promised to write once she settled in a position in Town.

Miranda longed to write more, but she knew it would not be safe. The less the Bentons knew, the less trouble for them should the truth about where she had been for the past week come out.

Propping the sealed letter up inside the desk, she closed the cover and started back to bed, hoping Sally would find the note when she dusted. As she was about to extinguish the candles, a soft rapping on her door caused her to draw her wrapper tightly around her. Her heart pounded with hope at who she longed for it to be. She padded to the door and cracked it slightly, then sighed with disappointment. Julian stood on the other side.

Pulling the door open, she stood quietly as Julian gestured for silence with his finger over his lips. He stole into the room, closing the door behind himself.

"I apologize for coming so late, but Charles stuck to me like a burr tonight. Do you still want to go to Town with me?"

"Yes, if you truly mean to go."

"Then be dressed and ready by five, for we must get on the road early. I shall tap on your door when I am ready to leave. It will be quite an adventure," Julian said with a great deal of bluster, as if to convince himself.

"Do you not wish to reconsider? You know Lord Cresswood will be dreadfully angry with you." Miranda felt the need to discourage the boy one last time.

"I am in his black books no matter what I do. I think you need my assistance."

Miranda was relieved Julian still intended to go despite the repercussions to himself. He truly was a brave lad.

With an encouraging tap under her chin, Julian moved to the door. "Don't worry so. All will be fine once we reach London. You will see. I have one more task to complete, then to bed for me as well."

"Until dawn, then," Miranda said as Julian saluted good night and cracked her door. He peered up and down the darkened hallway, then winked before closing the door softly behind him.

As Miranda climbed into bed, she wondered what else he must do tonight to prepare for the journey. She pushed away doubts about allowing Julian to involve himself in her problems. He was her only hope to get safely to Town. Pulling the covers up around her, she wished she could go to sleep and wake up from this bad dream.

Cold rain splashed upon the roof of the black carriage as it moved at a moderate pace towards East Grinstead. Miranda pulled the fur rug up as a sudden bounce of the carriage caused it to slide downward. She glanced at Julian's face in the pale grey light of the morning. While his mouth was set in a grim line as he peered into the falling rain, his eyes glowed with excitement.

The miserable weather did little to dampen his enthusiasm for an adventure. Even the absence of his groom, which puzzled Miranda, did not appear to discourage the young man from his escapade.

"Are you warm enough, Lady Miranda?" Julian inquired, using her real name with obvious glee.

"Quite. I only hope you won't catch a cold. It would

be one more thing for your brother to blame me for in this scheme."

"Why, I am mostly dry," Julian said as he brushed a few drops from his greatcoat.

"Good, for it would be a very shabby trick to repay your mother's kindness by dragging you to Town and allowing you to become ill," Miranda fretted.

"Don't worry, for I am rarely ill. We'll be in Town before darkness falls this evening. That is when it will truly become miserable."

The pair fell silent while Julian maneuvered the carriage through East Grinstead and turned north up the main pike to London. The rain lessened, but the coaching traffic increased as they continued up the main thoroughfare to Town.

"Blast," Julian uttered.

"Is there some problem?"

"My leader appears to have thrown a shoe. We shall have to stop at the nearest posting house and get a new team. Cresswood will forgive me anything but laming his horses." Julian's face was a picture of frustration as he slowed the team to a gentle walk.

Some thirty minutes later they came upon a bustling inn. Julian deftly drove the coach through the gates and past the vehicles clogging the yard. He pulled the carriage to a halt in front of the doorway and helped Miranda down as the rain renewed its heavy downpour.

Hurrying into the rear hall of the inn, Miranda paid scant attention to the numerous bucks who ogled her in the crowded taproom. She relished the warmth of the posting house after the damp morning drive.

Julian shouted for a private parlor for the lady and

some assistance with his team. When an ostler took his carriage in hand, Julian followed Miranda to await the landlord.

A thin scarecrow of a man arrived, eyeing the pair with doubt. As he took in Julian's expensive attire, his face took on a sunny appearance. He showed the pair into his remaining parlor, a low-ceilinged room with roaring fire. Miranda could tell by the winks and sly grin he cast at Julian that he suspected them of heading for Gretna Green.

Haughtily she eyed the man as Julian ordered tea and breakfast for his 'cousin' and himself. She was glad the young man owned the presence of mind to cover for her lack of a servant.

The innkeeper smirked, then bowed, leaving them alone. Miranda tossed her bonnet upon the bench by the window. "Julian, the farther we go, the more uncertain I am about this trip. You see how that man looks at us."

"The landlord? He is of no importance. You will feel much better about us leaving once you get a nice cup of hot tea in you. It will calm your nerves. Now, I must go and see about the horses. Pour me a cup when breakfast arrives, for we must get on the road as quickly as we can."

Fearfully, Miranda asked, "Do you think your brother will pursue us so soon?" She knew she would be unable to face the earl with that cold look in his eyes.

Julian patted her gloved hands. "Don't worry. It will be hours before anyone is aware you have left with me."

Miranda attempted a smile, but her heart was not in it. She watched as Julian strode from the room. With resignation, she walked to the small table in the center of the room and sat heavily on the wooden chair. As she pulled off her gloves, she decided there was little she could do to change things, for they could not go back now.

The tea arrived some minutes later with a harried maid who was as large as the landlord was thin. She eyed Miranda with curiosity as she dropped the tray unceremoniously on the table, then left, closing the parlor door with a slight bang.

As the aroma of the fresh-baked bread wafted to her, Miranda realized she was hungry despite her nerves. After pouring tea for them both, she began to butter a thick slice. She hoped Julian would soon return, for she drew strength from his confidence. As if her wish had been heard, Julian appeared at the door, shaking water from his beaver hat and tossing his greatcoat upon a chair at the door.

"We are in good shape. I arranged for a new team and the greys will be stabled here until I return." His buoyant mood made Miranda feel better.

Calmer, she enjoyed her tea and bread as Julian opted for a portion of ham and eggs as well. She passed him a plate of preserves and inquired, "Have you decided what you plan to do once you reach London?"

"I shall look up my old friend, Robbie Lightman. He has been in Town since October, when he was sent down. He is a lively chap and should let me stay in his rooms for a few days. I want to remain in Town and make certain you don't have any trouble from Lord Redford."

Smiling gratefully, Miranda said, "You know once I

get to Missy's I shall be safe. Sylvester will likely soon grow tired of searching for me."

"That may be, but I will feel much better if I keep an eye on you for a week or so."

"And what of your brother? He will be in a towering rage when he discovers you did not go to Southampton," Miranda worried.

"Once you are settled I will write to Charles and tell him your true story without giving him any names. That way you can remain safely hidden with your governess and I will be the hero of the story."

"I hope it shall turn out that way." Miranda wanted to believe things might be different for her as well once the truth was told, but she refused to dwell on her lost chances with the earl.

As Julian brushed the crumbs from his lap, he looked out the window. "It looks as if the rain is letting up. I think we must get on the road. The sooner we get to London, the safer you will be."

"I don't believe you will be going anywhere, my good fellow," a cold voice stated from the doorway.

"Sylvester!" Miranda uttered the name with revulsion.

Twelve

Rain pattered softly on the breakfast parlor windows at Oakhill Manor as Cresswood entered. Expecting to dine alone, the earl halted. His mother stood at the sideboard daintily selecting an egg from the large array of food.

"Good morning, Mother. You are up early. Is there some problem?" The earl tensed in the doorway. He'd stopped at Julian's room to confirm the boy had left for Southampton as instructed, but his mother's presence in the parlor concerned him that there was some unforeseen hitch in his brother's departure.

"No problem, merely Agatha and Reggie leaving this morning and I wanted to be up early to arrange a nice farewell breakfast." The dowager countess added two slices of toast to her plate before returning to the table.

Walking to the buffet, the earl surveyed the feast. "I hope Cook won't regret starting quite so early, for Reggie rarely appears before noon."

" 'Twas Reggie himself who informed me they would be gone by nine this morning. They wish to reach Chartley Hall before dark. Now, I must ask—what is all this about sending Julian to Southampton?" Lady Cresswood poured tea for them both.

"There is no cause for alarm, Mother. He is to inspect the changes being made on the yacht. He should be back in a few days. You know Jamie will keep an eye on him and prevent him from getting into trouble." The earl joined his mother at the table with a full plate, but avoided her penetrating gaze as he sat down.

"But I thought you drove down yourself last month. Indeed, I remember your saying all was as you wished it. Why send Julian out in such weather to look at something which you inspected already?" She eyed him with puzzled inquiry.

"Julian pays scant heed to the weather, Mother. He would scorn the suggestion he forgo some adventure for mere rain. As to the trip, I know the work on the boat is near completion and I want to make certain the workmanship is good quality before they sail back to home port. By the time he returns, we should have an answer from Halley regarding the West Indies trip."

"But why was Julian so angry about going?"

As Cresswood concentrated on cutting a slice of ham, he responded, "Because he wished to remain until Miss Hamilton continued her trip to Town. But she is much improved and I shall take her in a day or so. There was no need for him to be hanging around kicking up his heels and getting into mischief."

Lady Cresswood, looking at the earl over the rim of her cup, made no comment.

A tap at the door sounded and Sally stuck her head into the room when bade to enter. She scanned the room as if she searched for someone; then, disappointment showing on her face, she entered completely. "Lady Cresswood, I apologize for interruptin' your meal, but

Miss Hamilton is missin' from her room. I hoped maybe she came down for breakfast, but her bandbox is gone as well."

The earl's utensils clattered to his plate as the maid spoke. With a feeling of foreboding, he asked, "Have you searched the rest of the house, Sally?"

"She's no place to be found, your lordship."

Eyeing his mother with a look of 'I predicted such,' the earl rose and shouted for Miller. Thanking Sally, he dismissed her. After informing the butler he wanted the head groom at once, he stood rigidly staring out at the dreary skies, his breakfast forgotten. He was determined to get to the bottom of this, but he suspected Miss Hamilton and his brother were well on their way to London—or worse, Gretna Green. He felt as if he'd taken a blow to his midsection while sparring.

As they awaited the arrival of the groom, the earl bitterly said, "It cannot be a coincidence Miss Hamilton disappears at the same time that Julian left."

"True, but I think we should not jump to any conclusions," the dowager countess suggested, a shadow of worry in her eyes.

As time seemed to drag, the earl began to pace the breakfast parlor. He was surprised when a young stable lad named Pauly arrived. "Where is Cuthbert?"

The boy, tousled red hair standing on end, stood before the earl, twisting a wet hat in his hands. "My lord . . . sir . . . Mr. Cuthbert be with Mr. Julian's groom, Jamie. The lad's his nephe', sir, and he be powerful sick."

"You mean Julian left this morning with no groom?" Fury almost choked the earl.

The hat twisted into a tight knot as the frightened youth answered, "We didn't know nuthin' about no trip. Mr. Julian visited Jamie last evenin' but he didn't ask fer his curri'le, sir. The lads and me was surprised to see his prads gone this morn."

Since Cresswood realized the stable hands had been duped by Julian, his tone was civil despite his anger. "Run up to the gate, Pauly, and see if the gatekeeper was called for by my brother. Quickly, lad. I want to know which direction they headed."

Rushing from the room, the lad puffed with pride at the responsibility. He tugged his hat back in place.

The earl was left with the disturbing realization the chit truly was with his brother. Why else the subterfuge? And what the devil did Julian do to Jamie? Cresswood feared the worst was about to be realized.

"Well, Mother, what say you of your Miss Hamilton now?" The earl looked accusingly at the dowager countess.

"I must admit I am puzzled by Miss Hamilton's unusual departure, but I sensed something troubled her. Mayhap Julian plans to help her with whatever the problem is."

"Help? Miss Hamilton doesn't require help, only some of Julian's fortune." The earl clenched his teeth tighter.

Looking at her son with troubled eyes, the dowager countess spoke softly. "Charles, you often jump to conclusions where Julian is concerned, but you have never misread a situation so badly in all your years of guardianship. I would stake my life this is no elopement."

"But 'tis Julian's life and happiness we gamble with.

I intend to follow them and put a stop to his involvement with this woman."

Lady Cresswood opened her mouth as if to defend the pair of runaways when Pauly came dashing into the open door of the room. Miller followed at his heels, protesting the lad's rude intrusion. Cresswood held up his hand to silence the butler.

"Summers says"—the dripping lad gasped for breath—"he opened the gate near five this morn."

"Did he see which way the carriage went?" The earl held his breath as he awaited the answer.

"He says Lord Julian and the lady was agoin' east, fer the main pike, my lord."

The earl felt no satisfaction at being right. Indeed, anger was the only emotion he was aware of. His whole demeanor was stiff as he spoke. "Have my carriage and fastest horses out front in ten minutes, for I travel to Town immediately."

Leaden skies no longer poured rain as the earl sprang his horses on the main pike to London. He hoped the muddy roads had hindered his brother's driving to such a degree that he could overtake the pair before noon.

A flash of despair stabbed him at the thought he might miss the couple. Would he be able to bear seeing Miss Hamilton if she became his brother's wife? Would he not feel the need to possess her? The thought of her with another, even his brother, staggered Cresswood. He'd been a fool to think he could merely dismiss her from his mind.

Slowing his team as he neared a busy inn, he attempted to pass a rig driven by an aged gentlemen. He spotted Julian's curricle before the inn he passed, hitched with a team of horses he did not recognize. With deft skill, he reined his team in and executed a tight turn to arrive in the inn yard without nicking any of the numerous vehicles coming and going.

Shouting for the ostler to walk his steaming horses, the earl jumped down and strode into the inn. At once he noticed a crowd of servants around a door at the rear of the main hallway. With an uneasy feeling, he advanced toward the group, knowing Julian was there.

The servants parted as he made his way to the room. Entering, he paused to observe the scene. The innkeeper and a maid hovered over Julian, who lay on a bench near the window. His cravat was untied and his hair was wet as if recently doused with water.

Pushing himself into a sitting position, Julian said weakly, "I tell you I am fine."

"Ye must not rise as yet, sir." The innkeeper pushed Julian back to the bench. "Ye were unconscious when Millie found ye, lad."

"Might I be of assistance?" The earl was relieved to see his brother safe.

"Charles." The dazed boy seemed surprisingly pleased to see him.

Scanning the room, the earl did not see Miss Hamilton among the group who gaped at the scene. Was she responsible for Julian's condition?

The innkeeper ran his gaze over the elegant attire of the earl. Sensing a person of importance, the thin man moved away from the boy and towards the man. "Sir, we took care of the lad quick as me daughter found 'im.

'E be only a might bruised but we can't convince 'im not to be goin' out in this fearsome weather."

"I feel sure you did your best, my good man. Please send two tankards of your best ale and I shall take care of him." The earl dropped several coins into the thin man's hand as he scanned his injured brother.

As the innkeeper cleared the room of servants, Julian slowly rose to face the earl. The ravages of some violent encounter were evident in his swollen eye, and a trace of blood crusted at the corner of his mouth.

Frowning, the earl asked, "Where is your companion and how did you manage to get your cork drawn scarcely thirty miles from Oakhill?"

"We must go after her, Charles. That blackguard took her and must be halfway to Hastings by now." Julian unsteadily advanced until he stood directly in front of the earl.

"Hastings? Why to such a remote location? And who is this blackguard of whom we speak?"

" 'Tis where his estate is located." Julian began to sway as he spoke.

"Here, lad, sit down," Charles pulled a chair up for his brother.

"I shall be fine, but I fear Lord Redford is very handy with his fives." The maid knocked and entered with two large tankards as Julian spoke.

Handing Julian one of the pewter containers as he dismissed the maid, the earl said, "Drink this, it will help." His brother drank deeply before the earl asked, "What the devil does a coxcomb like Redford have to do with you or Miss Hamilton?"

"The Earl of Redford is Lady Miranda's brother." Julian spoke as if making all perfectly clear.

Feeling as if he were dealing with an escapee from Bedlam, the earl eyed his brother with doubt. "Who is Lady Miranda?"

Julian brought a hand up to test the swollen skin on his face. "Do you suppose I shall have a black eye?"

"You shall have two unless you clear up this mystery. Now, from the beginning. Who is Lady Miranda and how do you come to be with her instead of Miss Hamilton?"

"Good grief, the man must have rattled my brain completely. I sit here chattering about my eye and we need to be on the road. Lady Miranda *is* our Miss Hamilton."

The earl froze as he brought his own tankard up to drink. "Are you telling me that Miss Hamilton was not her true name?"

"Lord no, Charles. She is Lady Miranda Henley and she was escaping from her stepbrother, Lord Redford, who is her guardian. He is trying to gain control of Lady Miranda's fortune by marrying her to a friend of his in the army. She was on her way to London to join her retired governess, Miss Mary Hamilton, when I ran her down on the road. Wasn't it fortunate we were able to hide her?" Julian beamed up at Cresswood when he finished speaking.

The earl sat down heavily on the straight-backed chair. He felt as if all the air was suddenly gone from the room. His mind quickly reviewed all the terrible things he'd said to the delicately bred young woman he'd thought a swindler. His mother was right. He'd let the circumstances override his own common sense.

As her beautiful face flashed through his mind, he

realized he'd fallen in love with the girl, even thinking her a schemer. Now she'd fled his home only to be caught by a guardian who would sell her into a loveless marriage. A burning rage settled in his stomach as he thought of Lord Redford and the despicable bridegroom, whoever he might be.

"Where is Redford's estate? Is that where they were headed?" the earl demanded.

"Lady Miranda said the estate is Brownstone. I think it is west of Hastings. But I can only guess that is where he took her."

"I must use your carriage, for my horses are spent. Rest here until you feel able, and then return my carriage to Oakhill. I am going to Hastings." The earl strode from the room, with a shaken Julian following behind.

"I shan't be left out of this," the boy said as he grabbed his brother's arm in the inn hallway. "I brought her here, Charles, and then let him take her. You must allow me to go. She is my friend, too."

Looking at his brother's troubled face, Cresswood knew he was overwhelmed with relief that the boy cared about Mary only as a friend—or, he should say, Lady Miranda. He could not deny his brother a chance to help rescue the girl. "I shall drive."

Shouting for the innkeeper, Cresswood gave rapid instructions before climbing into Julian's carriage. His brother scarcely had time to get in before the curricle was bowling from the inn yard.

The sound of pounding hooves and the rocking of the carriage penetrated Miranda's drugged stupor. She thought she was going to be sick as the motion of the carriage rocked her around on the seat. Opening her eyes, she realized she was in Sylvester's traveling coach.

Memories of the events in the inn flooded back as she turned and eyed her stepbrother sitting across from her. He'd knocked Julian out and, with threats of further harm to the unconscious boy, forced her to drink some bitter concoction.

"Well, my dear, we are almost at Brownstone. I have the pleasure of informing you that you shall be married before the sun sets on this day. Herbert has the special license, and I will inform him of your return as soon as you are safely locked in your room." Sylvester's round face looked smug despite the dark circles around his eyes and the reddish-brown stubble on his chin.

Attempting to sit up, Miranda discovered her hands were tied with a strip of ribbon. She wondered how Sylvester had gotten her out of the inn. Looking back at her stepbrother, she realized he was deadly serious about keeping her from escaping again. It would be useless to try to get away until she reached her room. But what then?

Struggling, she rose to a sitting position as a new wave of nausea struck. For several minutes, she breathed deeply to control the sickness. Slowly the feeling passed.

Staring out the window, she recognized the passing landscape. They were a few miles from Brownstone, and she still had no plan. At least the rain had stopped, but the skies were still overcast.

"Might I ask where you came across that young cub from the inn?" Sylvester rubbed his chin where Julian had struck him before being bested by the larger man.

"He was just a kind gentleman who helped me along the road. I would advise you keep an eye upon your back, for Lord Cresswood might take exception to your harming his brother." Miranda kept her gaze on the window, but worried about her young friend. Would Cresswood blame her for Julian's injuries? Would he come to avenge his brother? Would he think of her? Her heart ached when she thought of never seeing the earl again.

"Cresswood! Well, I might have something to say to that too proud gentleman about his brother abducting my ward. Am I to understand you have been under his protection for this past week?"

"I really don't care what you understand."

"It makes no difference to me or Herbert. He cares more for your fortune than your virtue." Sylvester spoke cruelly.

Miranda didn't respond, for she was well aware of what both men wanted. She ignored the few comments her stepbrother continued to offer until he fell silent, leaving her time to plan.

Except for her maid Jenny, who'd aided her in her previous escape, the servants would not help her. She would have to allow them to lock her in her room, but once there, what could she do? Brownstone was a relatively modern building with none of the secret passages or priest holes of some of the older homes. It had been built by Sylvester's grandfather.

As the image of the building came to mind, she suddenly remembered an incident which had occurred when she first came to the manor. The ten-year-old Miranda had been fascinated with the ornate decoration which adorned each corner of the building. The builder had formed a pattern of every other block protruding several inches from the wall face, creating a ridged design up the side of the building. She had seen the pattern as an enticing ladder and climbed up to the second floor before Missy had arrived to hysterically call her down. She had been forbidden to ever climb on the building again, but she remembered how easy it had seemed. Could she use it to climb down?

As the carriage turned in at Brownstone, Sylvester reached over to untie the band which held her hands. "I could not risk your trying to get away while I stopped to refresh myself, but I think you might prefer to be free now for your wedding."

She knew he did not wish the servants to see the bindings, but made no comment. Her mind was busy planning her escape. She knew it would be dangerous, but she was determined to thwart Sylvester and Herbert. At least if she fell to her death, her fortune would revert to the unknown distant relative who had inherited her father's title. But she would not think of that, only of succeeding.

The coach stopped and the door was opened by Hatcher. "Welcome home, my lord."

Miranda held her head high, looking neither left nor right at the servants who stared as she came down from the coach. She felt weak and sick, but she was determined to make it to her room unaided.

"Hatcher, escort Lady Miranda to her room and remain outside her door until Major Caldwell arrives." Sylvester climbed back into the coach and ordered the coachman to Swallowford.

"This way, my lady," Hatcher said, a hint of apology in his gruff voice.

"Might I have Jenny bring me tea and help me change for my . . . wedding?" Miranda looked down at her crumpled traveling gown, which she had donned that morning as if she were concerned about her appearance.

Hatcher gave the order, then gestured for Miranda to precede him up the stairway. He followed quickly behind her as she made her way to the chamber she'd hoped never to see again.

Some minutes later Jenny arrived with tea and sandwiches, her face full of distress. "Oh, my lady, I hoped you would make it to Town."

"Jenny, 'tis good to see you unharmed. I worried Lord Redford might turn you off after I left." Miranda came forward and hugged the young maid after she set the tray upon the table.

"Me? I'm fine. His lordship never suspected I helped you. When Major Caldwell arrived that night—quite foxed, I might add—there was such an uproar when they discovered you missing no one thought to ask how you got out. But sad I am to see you, and peaked you're lookin'."

"Jenny, I have little time. Will you find me a spare set of clothes from one of the footmen?" Miranda began to undo the blue jacket of her gown.

"You be wanting livery, my lady?" Jenny's face showed shock at the suggestion her mistress would don men's clothing.

"Yes, and hurry. Sylvester is returning with the major shortly and I must get away." Miranda's face was set, allowing for no argument from the maid.

Jenny returned some minutes later with a bundle containing a pair of worn brown pants and greyish shirt with a leather vest. " 'Twas the best I could do, my lady. What are you plannin'?"

"Open that window, Jenny." Miranda pointed to one of the large windows as she donned the pants.

"Oh, my lady, you're not thinkin' of jumpin'. I won't allow it." Jenny stood frozen with shock.

"Don't be silly, Jenny. Of course not. Open the window and look to the left."

The young maid reluctantly walked over to open the window. Sticking her head out she called, "I don't see nuthin', my lady."

Buttoning the vest, which smelled of horses, Miranda walked to the window and gestured at the raised blocks which extended down the length of the corner. "When I was a child, I was able to climb up and down those."

The maid's eyes grew round. "Lady Miranda, it'll be very dangerous. I wish you'd think up another plan."

"There is no time. Sylvester will be back any minute. I must go now while there is still light."

Clutching at her mistress, Jenny argued, "I don't like it. I got a bad feelin' about you climbin' 'round out there."

As Miranda stared out at the ground far below, she was nervous but confident. The sound of a carriage coming up the drive made her heart pound with panic. It must be Sylvester.

With trembling hands, she grasped the windowsill and thought of the earl. How could she exist in a marriage with a man like Caldwell, when Cresswood was always going to be in her heart and mind? "I must go, Jenny. I shall never marry the major, for my heart belongs to another."

Thirteen

Reentering the carriage at the Golden Hart, the earl tersely announced, "The landlord said Redford's manor is but two miles ahead past the small stream."

"I shall darken his daylights when I see his scruffy face," Julian threatened for the fifth time, before adding thoughtfully, "I pray Brownstone is where they were going." Then he guided the curricle out of the inn's yard, having taken over the driving at the last change of horses.

Agreeing, Cresswood fell silent as the team picked up speed. His stomach knotted as he thought about Lady Miranda. It had taken much of the trip for him to think of her by that name. Now his mind dwelled on his stubborn conviction she was a lightskirt and swindler. Why had he refused to believe what was before his eyes as he watched her behaving with gentility and kindness? His own family had welcomed her and seen her true value, while he, on the flimsiest of evidence, had condemned her. Because of such folly, he might lose the woman he realized meant more to him than his own life. His hand gripped the side of the coach as that thought swirled through his brain.

Two moss-covered stone lions silently greeted them

as Julian turned the curricle into the gate of Brownstone. As they tooled up the driveway, the earl saw two men step down from a carriage. A military uniform alerted him he was looking at the man who wished to wed Miranda. The disheveled companion he recognized as Redford. A deep fury burned in his soul. He clenched his hands into fists as rage surged through him.

Scanning their faces, the earl knew he must keep tight control of his temper. But every fiber of his being longed to extract revenge upon the scoundrels who would take Miranda from him.

As the gentlemen turned to view the approaching carriage, there was no welcome in either man's face. Indeed, Lord Redford's expression was decidedly hostile.

The earl jumped to the ground before the carriage came to a complete stop. Striding deliberately toward the pair under the portico, he set his face in a lofty mask. The sound of Julian's steps ringing on the cobblestones behind him worried him only slightly as he concentrated on the blackguards on the stairs.

"Lord Redford." Cresswood kept his voice cold and condescending.

"So, Cresswood, you dare show your face here after allowing your brother to cavort with my sister this past week?" Sylvester placed his hands on his hips. As he shifted his gaze to Julian, there was indignation on his unshaven face.

Several footmen hovered behind the thickset man awaiting the party's entrance into the manor. They stood wide-eyed with curiosity as they sensed the tension in the visitors.

The major, now standing in front of the doorway with

his back to the newcomers, peered into the open portal as if searching for his prey. The callers appeared to be of little interest to him.

"I believe you are already acquainted with my brother." The earl did not pause for the pair to exchange greetings. "I came to bring my fiancee, Lady Miranda, back to my estate and the protection of my mother," the earl prevaricated with a curt bow as his brother stood close by.

The only sign of surprise Julian showed at the startling statement was a widening of his eyes before he parroted, "Must return her to our mother at Oakhill."

"Here now, Redford, what kind of trick is this?" Major Caldwell blustered, turning to face his companion with sudden attention. "I thought all was settled in this matter."

"And so it is." Redford glared at Cresswood. "You and your brother have no business interfering with the plans for my stepsister, sir."

Keeping a rein on his anger, the earl looked at Miranda's stepbrother with disdain. "I think you forgot the lady's welfare while making your . . . plans."

Extending his arm towards the major, Redford countered, "This is Miranda's fiancee. Major Caldwell."

"Caldwell? I have never heard of the family," the earl said dismissively.

The major stiffened with offense at the earl's tone. "The Caldwells are an old and respected family, sir. There can be no objection to such a match."

Sensing the major was the weaker opponent, the earl addressed him. "In Society's eyes, mayhap not, but what of the lady herself? I would think having a bride who would promote your career in the army might be preferable to one who is indifferent to your profession."

Frowning, the major responded, "There are many considerations when choosing a wife, sir."

"Ah, yes, we speak of fortune. But what good will the income do if you ruin your career taking such a step? I would dislike going to the Horse Guard and speaking with my friend the Duke of York about you, sir, but . . ." The earl allowed his voice to trail off, leaving his threat to the major's imagination.

Rounding on Redford, the major hissed, "This scheme of yours and Grandfather's is now at an end. I would not give up my career for him, and I'll certainly not give it up for some unwilling chit simply for the money. There are too many heiresses on the tree to pick one which is sour."

Major Caldwell bowed stiffly to the gentlemen, but his gaze lingered hostilely on Cresswood a moment longer. Without further comment, the soldier marched down the stairs to the Redford carriage and ordered the coachman to return him to Swallowford.

As the vehicle moved up the drive, Cresswood looked back at Redford. "I should very much like to see *my* fiancee, Redford."

The round face of Miranda's brother flushed and his eyes narrowed as he gazed back with dislike. "Not so fast, Cresswood. You have whistled down an excellent match for my stepsister. I will not allow you—"

Cresswood's hand shot out and grasped the man's cravat. He dragged him down the stairs to stand face to face with him. Looking down into Redford's dazed eyes, the earl spoke softly, menacingly. "I will not mention

Lady Miranda's fleeing your home in fear during the night. I will not mention my brother being attacked and abandoned at a posting house, for if we discuss those matters I might feel the need to call you out, Redford."

"No, no, I mistook your brother—"

The earl's control slipped and he tightened his grip. Nearly shouting, he spat out, "I *said* we will not speak of these matters. I wish to see Lady Miranda . . . at once."

As a gasping Redford struggled to breathe, Julian darted forward. Grabbing his brother's hands, he loosened them from the red-faced man's cravat. "Charles, think of Miranda. It would be a scandal if you killed her stepbrother."

Realizing Julian was correct, Cresswood released the cur. He glanced at his brother with surprise. The boy had been all bravado in the carriage about what he would do to Redford. Now, seeing his older brother lose control, he'd made the mature choice. "You are right, Julian. Thank you."

Taking a calming breath, the earl looked back at Miranda's stepbrother. "I can be a powerful enemy or a strong ally in Town, Redford. Allying yourself with the Bentons is no small matter if you plan to continue to move in Society. Do you comprehend my meaning, sir?"

Little did the earl want to reward this blackguard, but, as his brother reminded him, his main thoughts must be for Miranda and getting her safely back to Oakhill. Julian had saved him from his own anger.

As he rubbed his throat with a shaking hand, Redford gave Cresswood a measuring look. A variety of expressions passed over Sylvester's round countenance as his emotions seemingly warred with one another. Finally, with a tone of resignation, he said, "Yes, I understand. I suggest we go in out of the cold and come to—"

Screams suddenly pierced the grey afternoon. Cresswood jerked his head in the direction of the sound, knowing at least one voice belonged to Miranda. His heart pounding, he rushed to the corner of the building, halting so quickly at the frightening sight before him that Julian bumped into his back.

Lying on a mulched leaf bed beside a brackish pool lay a trouser-clad figure. Cresswood would have thought it a boy except for the familiar golden curls spread upon the turf. She lay frighteningly still and quiet. Panic as he'd never known before surged through him.

On the second floor, a young girl wearing a mobcap continued to shriek from the open window. She babbled hysterically at her mistress below.

With an icy feeling around his heart, Cresswood moved forward, gaining speed with each stride. He stepped off the path into the flower bed. As the spongy soil near the empty fish pond sank under his boot, he prayed the soft ground had prevented serious harm.

The sounds of boots on the stone path vaguely penetrated his thoughts as Julian, the footmen, and a huffing Redford came up the walk behind him. His brother held the men back to allow Charles some measure of privacy as he gestured for them to stop.

Miranda's eyes were closed and her complexion ghostly pale as Cresswood knelt beside her. Touching her ivory cheek with shaking fingers, the earl whispered, "I cannot live without you, my love."

The young maid ceased her wailing. She called, "Take care of her, sir."

Cresswood gently lifted Miranda's head. In a voice hoarse with emotion, he pleaded, "Dear heart, please open your eyes."

Deep in her darkness, Miranda struggled to take a breath. The impact had stunned her so, she could find no air to replace all that was lost when she struck the ground. As she strained to draw in the much-needed air, she heard a soothing voice far away.

With a concentrated effort, she gasped in the damp air. The pain in her chest lessened, and she reached out to clutch the one who held her. She knew she was safe and comfortable in those strong arms.

Remembering where she was, her eyes flew open with fear. Gazing down at her with deep concern was Lord Cresswood. She blinked to make sure it truly was the earl. She gave him a small, tremulous smile as she relaxed into the strong arms which pulled her close, and her heart pounded with joy as she gazed into slate eyes filled with some deep emotion.

"Lady Miranda, tell me you are not injured." The earl's hand caressed her cheek.

How could the earl be here and calling her by her real name? She murmured with confusion, "I am not sure, my lord. I believe the fall merely knocked the breath from me. But how do you come to be here, sir?"

"Julian told me your true identity. Was I so terrible you could not confide in me?" The earl's mouth turned down with wounded pride.

"Julian! How is he? Where is he?" Miranda crushed the material of the earl's greatcoat in fear. She did not wish to answer his question, for he'd often been unapproachable at Oakhill.

"The boy's fine. In truth, I have been wishing him in the Indies these last fifty miles for all his dire threats to your stepbrother. Then I found 'twas I who was doing all the dire things and Julian was stopping me." Cresswood sounded embarrassed by his loss of composure.

Miranda was relieved as Julian stepped into view and gazed at her with worried eyes.

"Sylvester?" Miranda breathed the name with trepidation. She glanced behind the earl to see her frowning stepbrother watching her from the path, then shrank back into the comforting arms of the earl.

"Don't worry about Lord Redford. He has come to see your side of the dispute. Now, do you think you can stand?" The earl gently helped Miranda to rise.

A mild pain throbbed when she placed her weight on her foot. "I fear I have reinjured my ankle."

"Well, I know an excellent place to recover. There is a room awaiting you and some wonderful nurses who have come to love you as much as I do."

Miranda merely stared at the earl, doubting her own ears.

Covering her cold hand with his own, the earl said, "Redford agreed with me about a substitution in bridegrooms, if the bride is willing. I can handle anything if I know you will be mine."

Her heart jolted and her pulse raced. Miranda dropped her gaze to the earl's white cravat, studying it intently. "Major Caldwell is gone?"

"Yes, he is. Dearest Miranda, I wish to have you with

me for all time. I want to take you back to Oakhill to-night. Will you be my wife, beloved?"

"Wife?" Miranda murmured with joy as her gaze took in every feature of his handsome face.

"If you will have me, my love. I have behaved like every kind of fool, but I love you to distraction. Do you think you could forgive me?" The earl held her close as he whispered his proposal.

"Yes, oh, yes. I do love you." She tilted her head back to receive his kiss. A delightful shiver ran through her as his lips covered hers.

Wrapping her arms around Cresswood's neck, Miranda lost herself in the earl's embrace. A muffled cough from the path reminded her they were not alone.

The earl reluctantly lifted his head and glanced back at his brother. "Julian, help me get Miranda out of this damp. We have a long trip back to Oakhill tonight."

Julian joined them. "Are you unharmed, Miranda?"

"I slightly hurt my ankle again. And you?" she asked.

"I'm fine. Cresswood informs me I have a splendid black eye, which will impress all the fellows at Oxford." Julian touched the swollen orb with pride.

Miranda looked fearfully at her stepbrother, who now stood eyeing the trio with a disgruntled face. "Are you sure Sylvester will permit me to marry as I wish? He is my legal guardian."

Drawing her close to him, the earl said, "Never fear, my love. I shall handle Redford henceforth."

Gazing into the earl's resolute face, Miranda felt safe and loved. It seemed like a miracle that he was here and he loved her as she did him. "I should be delighted to allow you to handle my stepbrother."

Julian eyed Redford as he asked, "Do you suppose we could get something to eat before we set off again? It doesn't look as if Charles has his wits about him at the moment."

Safely tucked in the earl's embrace, Miranda asserted herself. "I will order refreshments for you while Jenny helps me pack." With hesitation, she queried, "Do you mean for me to go with you to Oakhill tonight?"

"I shall not leave here without you," the earl stated emphatically.

"Wake up, my love. We are at Oakhill," the earl spoke into the darkened coach.

Miranda's lovely face appeared at the window, eyes twinkling in the shaft of light from the open door of the manor. "We are awake. Jenny wished to see her new home, if only by moonlight, Charles."

Opening the door of the vehicle, the earl helped Miranda and her maid down. He was still surprised at the difference in his love. Her attire was elegant, if not of the latest fashion. She held a grey fur muff, which matched the fur on the collar of her rose cloak. But the most obvious difference was the dazzling look she bestowed upon him. "Then may I welcome you to your new home, my dear?"

"We are delighted to be here, sir." Miranda curtsied playfully despite the late hour and her obvious fatigue.

The earl turned to the hovering butler. "Miller, please have all the trunks taken up to Lady Miranda's room. Also find a place for her maid, Jenny. She will be joining our staff."

An uncharacteristic tilt of his head was the only indication of surprise the butler showed as he replied. "Very good, my lord."

Jenny stepped from behind Miranda and spoke fearfully. "You won't be forgettin' yer promise to have my mum brung up from Hastings, my lord?"

"No, Jenny. I owe you a very large debt for aiding Lady Miranda's escape the first time. Without you, I would never have met my love."

The maid swelled with pride as she followed Miller into the manor.

The earl reached out and took Miranda's gloved hand, giving it a loving squeeze as he brought it to rest on his arm. Watching her lovely face, he saw a shadow of worry as she glanced through the door.

"How do you think your mother will react to the news? I hope she will be able to forgive my deceiving your family," Miranda worried.

"My mother had faith in you when I was so desperately trying to convince myself you were a schemer. Don't worry, for she has more heart than almost anyone I know." The earl pressed a kiss to Miranda's forehead with lingering enjoyment.

As he led her inside, he savored the feel of her hand upon his arm. He would be glad to have a moment alone with her later to show her what she meant to him.

His mother stood in the Great Hall, looking anxious for news of her sons. Ellen hovered behind her. Both ladies smiled as they saw the earl and his companions.

"Where is Julian?" the dowager countess asked as her eyes searched the dark doorway.

"He took his curricle and Lady Miranda's horse,

Baruq, which we retrieved, round to the stables. He felt he owned Jamie an apology for the nasty trick he played upon him to get away this morning. He will be here soon," the earl reassured her.

The dowager countess smiled. "Jamie was much impressed that Julian was able to hoax him. The lad assured me it shan't happen again. I told him not to worry, for no one blamed him."

The earl merely nodded his head. He would visit the groom on the morrow, he decided. For now his thoughts were on telling his family the truth about Miranda.

"Mother," Cresswood said, as he led a limping Miranda forward, "I would very much like to formally introduce you to my fiancee, Lady Miranda Henley. She is the daughter of the late Earl of Manville."

The dowager countess gave her son a knowing look as she smiled her approval. Then, turning to Miranda, she said, "So you are my dear Olivia's daughter. How delightful!"

Removing her bonnet, Miranda said, "Yes, I wanted to tell you when you spoke of my mother. Please forgive my deception, Lady Cresswood. I fear my stepbrother was trying to force a horrid marriage upon me. I thought it best you call me by my governess's name when I awoke and discovered you thought me to be Mary."

Taking Miranda's hands, the dowager countess smiled. "I suspected some mystery, but I knew you to be a lady of breeding, my dear. I welcome you to the family with delight."

"Oh, we are to be sisters!" Ellen came and kissed Miranda's pink cheek.

"Peter!" The earl spotted his friend standing quietly

near the open drawing room door. Walking over to Weldon he asked, "When did you arrive?"

Stepping forward, the baronet spoke in a low tone. "I arrived in time to share a delightful meal with your mother and sister. I came as soon as I returned from the north. Where is Mary Hamilton and my five hundred pounds?"

Laughing, the earl clapped his friend on the shoulder and said, "I don't know where your Mary is, but come and meet mine."

The earl drew his friend toward his fiancee. "My dear, this is Sir Peter Weldon, an old friend. Peter, this is my fiancee, Lady Miranda Henley. She is *my* Mary, but it is a long story."

"Sir Peter, I am delighted to meet you, and I am so sorry you came all this way for the wrong Miss Hamilton. Charles explained who he thought I was when we were at Brownstone. It would seem that my old governess has the same name as your lady friend." Miranda looked lovingly up at the earl.

Taking her hand, Sir Peter bowed gallantly. "I would gladly travel all this way for such wonderful news."

"I hope you will remain, for we plan to be married by the end of the week." The earl placed his arm around Miranda as he spoke.

"I should be delighted." Weldon smiled.

"But I have forgotten," the earl said. "How is your mother, and did you recover the emeralds?"

With a look of relief, Peter answered, "Mother has completely recuperated now that she has her necklace back. They caught the fellows just outside of Town. 'Twas a relief to have it all settled so quickly."

As the group discussed the robbery, the door opened to reveal Julian. He strode forward and kissed his mother's cheek. "We've had a splendid adventure, Mother."

Touching his swollen eye, the dowager countess said, "So it would appear. I hope this is the worst of the injuries."

"Yes, 'tis the merest trifle. I will be the envy of my friends," Julian bragged. "Now we are to have a wedding. It should be great fun."

The dowager countess smiled before turning to Cresswood. "You might wish to call on the vicar at once. Mr. Halley was here this afternoon and said the reverend was going to Brighton for a brief visit soon. The curate informed me he was at your disposal after the first of the year."

With a glint of amusement, the earl looked at Julian. "Now that all is settled, I believe you made me a promise about returning to school willingly if I allowed you to remain."

Julian glanced around the group with sad eyes. "I guess I am off to Oxford after the wedding."

"You need to get back as soon as possible," the earl announced.

Fingering a button on his coat, Julian looked miserable. "Can't I leave right after the wedding?"

"But, Charles . . ." Miranda started to protest.

The earl silenced her with a gesture. His eyes twinkling, he spoke to his brother. "Yes, right after the wedding you must be on the road, Julian."

A stunned silence fell over the company before the earl continued. "I want all your belongings packed and returned here by Christmas. And don't forget to give up your rooms as well, for I have no idea how long you will be traveling."

Looking up suddenly, Julian grinned back at his brother. "Do you mean it? I can go to the West Indies?"

"Yes, in the new year," the earl smiled.

Julian grabbed Ellen and began to twirl her around the front hall as if he were waltzing. The pair laughed delightedly.

Miranda smiled up at the earl. "I knew you would agree to the trip."

With a kiss upon her lovely ear, the earl whispered, "I want to have some peace and quiet with my bride and not have to worry about Julian's scrapes. I shall let the curate bear-lead him for a while."

Cresswood watched his siblings indulgently with a feeling of satisfaction. Then, realizing the hour, he thought it best to end this celebration. "Julian, we shall make all the plans tomorrow. Now I think we need to retire. It is getting late."

Lady Cresswood took over her duties as hostess. "Yes, Julian, you will wake Cousin Amelia with your revels. Miranda, you shall be in your old room."

Julian and Ellen wished everyone good night as Sir Peter followed them up the stairs. The earl clutched Miranda's hand when she moved to leave.

Cresswood also detained his mother for a moment as well. "Did Reggie and Aunt Agatha leave?"

"Yes, dearest. I thought it best to allow them to depart without informing them of your 'adventure.' I believe Agatha is in enough shock with the changes in Reggie. She has barely spoken in the last two days. It was quite the most delightful visit we have ever had. Now, I shall leave you to say your good night privately." The dowager countess kissed her son and future daughter-in-law, then went up the stairs.

Miranda smiled. "Your mother is a very wise lady."

Leading Miranda into the drawing room, the earl encircled her with his arms. "Yes, she is, for she realized I loved you even when I kept denying it. I can only say that I am grateful you are as forgiving as your namesake."

"My namesake?"

"Yes, from *The Tempest*. 'Admired Miranda. Indeed the top of admiration, worth what's dearest to the world!'" Charles quoted the lines from Shakespeare before adding some of his own. "Dearest to *my* world, my love."

Miranda laughed. "How could I not forgive the man I loved? He has forgiven me."

"May I now show you how much I do love you?"

"Please," Miranda whispered as her arms came round his neck and her lips met his.

ABOUT THE AUTHOR

Lynn Collum lives with her family in Florida. She is the author of four Zebra Regency romances. She is currently working on her fifth, *An Unlikely Father,* which will be published in December, 1999. Lynn loves to hear from her readers and you may write to her at P.O. Box 478, DeLand, FL 32724. Please include a self-addressed stamped envelope if you wish a response.

BOOK YOUR PLACE ON OUR WEBSITE AND MAKE THE READING CONNECTION!

We've created a customized website just for our very special readers, where you can get the inside scoop on everything that's going on with Zebra, Pinnacle and Kensington books.

When you come online, you'll have the exciting opportunity to:

- View covers of upcoming books
- Read sample chapters
- Learn about our future publishing schedule (listed by publication month *and author*)
- Find out when your favorite authors will be visiting a city near you
- Search for and order backlist books from our online catalog
- Check out author bios and background information
- Send e-mail to your favorite authors
- Meet the Kensington staff online
- Join us in weekly chats with authors, readers and other guests
- Get writing guidelines
- AND MUCH MORE!

Visit our website at
http://www.zebrabooks.com